QUARTER TO MIDNIGHT

Brutally attacked one night in the woods, Steve Karner hadn't been seen in years, and everyone in the Oregon town of Stayton thought him dead. Then the men who tried to kill him start dying, one by one; and it soon becomes apparent that Karner is not only alive, but riding a vengeance trail. But there are many dangers to be faced along the way, including a cunning young millionaire who will use all his family's power to protect his secrets, and a cold-blooded hired killer out for Karner's blood . . .

NED OAKS

QUARTER TO MIDNIGHT

Complete and Unabridged

LINFORD
Leicester

First published in Great Britain in 2016 by
Robert Hale
an imprint of The Crowood Press
Wiltshire

First Linford Edition
published 2019
by arrangement with
The Crowood Press
Wiltshire

A catalogue record for this book is available
from the British Library.

ISBN 978–1–4448–4176–3

Published by
F. A. Thorpe (Publishing)
Anstey, Leicestershire

Set by Words & Graphics Ltd.
Anstey, Leicestershire
Printed and bound in Great Britain by
T. J. International Ltd., Padstow, Cornwall

1

Moonlight reflected off the windows of the carriage as the train moved through the night. It had departed from Bend a little after ten o'clock, heading west toward Salem. There were only a few people on board in the three passenger cars. Nearly all were sleeping as the powerful locomotive chugged its way through the darkness to the Oregon capital.

Jack Buckley had been very drunk for hours before he got on the train. He was sitting toward the front of the last passenger car, dozing fitfully. Occasionally he would awaken and pull the flask of whiskey from the pocket of his heavy sheepskin coat, treating himself to a healthy swig. Drops of rotgut dripped from the whiskers on his chin. When he looked out of the window, all he saw was the dark outline of the tree-cloaked ridges, and sometimes he looked down into the yawning canyons that bordered the railroad tracks.

He belched loudly and sat up straighter in his seat. They still had about three hours before the train reached Salem. He thumbed his Stetson to the back of his head and glanced over his shoulder at the other passengers. An elderly couple was sleeping in their seats about halfway back in the car. The woman had her head on the man's shoulder, and his head was leaning up against the window, his mouth agape as he snored. Buckley twisted a little in his seat and looked toward the back. A young man with a thick beard sat in the last row of seats, his black hat pulled down over his face. He appeared to be asleep, too. There was no one else in the carriage.

Buckley yawned, his hand moving reflexively toward the flask in his pocket. But he stopped himself, realizing that if he kept drinking like he was, he would be out of whiskey long before he reached Salem. Better to ration it, he thought. I'm drunk enough. For now, anyway.

He had spent two days in Bend, drinking and gambling in the town's saloons with his brother. He had had such a good time that he almost stayed another day, but he knew he couldn't linger if he wanted to keep his job at the lumber mill in Stayton, fifteen miles east of Salem. At twenty-six, he was one of the top men at the mill, which was the largest in that area of the Willamette Valley.

Buckley put his head back against the seat and tried to sleep again. His stomach was bothering him, precluding slumber. Maybe it's better that I left Bend after all, he thought. Too much whiskey in too little time. When it came to drinking, he was prone to overdoing it. He chuckled as he thought of the time he had spent with his brother. They had played lots of poker, dallied with some saloon whores, and gotten into a few fights, each of which they had won handily. Buckley prided himself on his skills as a fighter; he was strong and good with his fists. He had a reputation for being intimidating, and even his friends watched their mouths around him.

A sudden wave of nausea washed over him. He was sweating. He thought fresh air and a smoke would help him feel better. He pushed himself up to his feet, swaying slightly, then turned around and began making his way toward the back of the car, using the tops of the seats to steady himself.

The wheels rattled on the tracks as he stumbled along. The old couple didn't stir as he passed them. He paused momentarily halfway down the carriage and fingered a cheroot from the inside pocket of his coat. He continued along and presently reached the back door. He flicked his eyes to the man who sat in the seat beside the door. He was a big man, lean but muscular. The brim of his hat was still pulled down over his face, but Buckley thought there was something vaguely familiar about the stranger. He considered the thought for a moment, and then his stomach lurched again.

He twisted the door handle and stepped onto the narrow platform. The wind was almost shocking in its briskness, but he welcomed it after the relative stuffiness of the carriage. He turned to his right, put his hands on the rail, and leaned out, much more alert than he had been only seconds before. The desire to vomit left him and he breathed deeply, watching the passing firs. He pushed the cheroot between his lips and scraped a match on the side of his pants, shielding it from the wind with a cupped hand. He sucked in the rich smoke and leaned a shoulder against the back wall of the carriage, already feeling better.

He was so relaxed he didn't hear the door of the rail car open. When it slammed shut, Buckley started and turned around irritably. Standing behind him on the platform was the stranger in the black hat. The man smiled and nodded at him, and again Buckley thought he knew him from somewhere.

'Nice night, ain't it?' the man asked amiably.

'I guess,' said Buckley with a sneer. He wasn't in the mood for company, and besides, he didn't like how the man had come upon him unawares. He turned his back and looked again at the passing trees.

'You got a light?' the stranger asked, seemingly oblivious to Buckley's disinterest in conversation.

Buckley looked over his shoulder at the man, who now held a large black cigar between his teeth. He thought about saying something, but instead chose to ignore him. The nausea had left his belly, but he still didn't feel very well. He looked back over the rail just as the tracks came alongside a deep river canyon. Moonlight glinted on the water far below.

Buckley stood up straight. He didn't like heights. So when he felt three hard taps in the center of his back, pushing him forward toward the rail, he was instantly enraged. He turned toward the stranger, his eyes blazing.

'What in hell you think you're doing?' he roared.

The other man grinned behind his thick black beard. Through his whiskey-sodden haze, Buckley thought the smile wasn't entirely friendly.

'I asked you a question,' the man said evenly. 'Thought maybe you didn't hear me.'

Something about the voice struck Jack Buckley, raising the hairs on the back of his neck.

'Don't go putting your hands on me, feller,' Buckley snarled. 'If you know what's good for you.'

He glared hard at the man and then turned, his hand reaching for the door handle. The stranger's right hand shot out just as Buckley began to turn the knob. His fingers encircled Buckley's wrist and squeezed, sending shooting pains up the drunken logger's forearm.

'Be damned!' Buckley cried, bringing up his right elbow toward the man's throat.

The stranger blocked the blow with his shoulder. He tightened his grip on Buckley's wrist and swung him around, shoving him toward the rail. At the same time, he pulled Buckley's arm up sharply behind his back, forcing a cry of pain from a man who had never before been physically dominated in such a fashion. He reached down and pulled Buckley's pistol from its holster, putting it into the waist of his own pants.

The stranger leaned toward Buckley, whose face was now glistening with sweat.

'You going to answer my question, friend?' he asked through clenched teeth.

'What?' Buckley whimpered, his eyes bulging as he stared down into the canyon below. 'What was the question?'

The stranger released the pressure on Buckley's arm, but only slightly.

'I asked if you had a light.'

Buckley's eyes were watering from the pain. He blinked some of the water away and said, 'Yeah, yeah — I got a light. I got some matches in my pocket. My left pocket.' He felt a hand go into the pocket of his sheepskin and quickly withdraw. Then the man released his arm and stepped back.

Buckley turned and stared at the man as the latter lighted his cigar. His own hands were trembling, but he noticed the stranger's hands were perfectly steady. He had a powerful urge to attack, and it was with a certain inner bafflement that he refrained from doing so. The man was only a few inches shorter than Buckley, who much preferred hitting smaller people.

'You don't remember me, do you?'

The question jarred Buckley back to reality. He squinted toward the man, whose face was illuminated by the burning tip of his huge cigar. His eyes stared back at Jack Buckley with complete self-assurance.

Something about the eyes sparked a

memory in Buckley. A cold tingle snaked down his back. He tried to dismiss the thought, because it was impossible. Yes — impossible. But . . .

'I don't know you, feller,' Buckley rasped, rubbing his sore arm.

The stranger pulled hard on his cigar and the tip glowed brightly. He reached up and removed it from his lips, letting the smoke trickle slowly out of his mouth.

'You know me,' he said. 'In fact, you helped kill me.'

Buckley's eyes widened, his heart pounding against his ribcage.

'Karner . . . ' he said softly. 'Steve Karner.'

Karner smiled. 'That's right,' he said. 'Steve Karner.'

'But — ' Buckley muttered.

'You thought I was dead, didn't you?' Karner asked.

'Yes.'

'Of course you did. As I recall, you did your best to make sure I was dead.'

'How did you survive?' Buckley

asked, almost despite himself.

'I don't know,' Karner responded. 'I guess I'm just tougher than you thought I was. And tougher than I thought I was, too.'

Buckley was nearing panic, and his face showed it.

'I only did what I was told,' he said. 'You've got to believe me.'

'Oh, I believe you. You always were nothing but a pathetic little worm, Jack. With a big mouth to boot.' Karner examined the tip of his cigar for a moment, letting his words settle in. 'I want to know who gave the orders.' He raised his head, his gaze locking on Buckley's face.

Buckley shrugged and shook his head. 'All I know is that Pete Taylor came to us and said we'd lose our jobs if we refused. He said you had crossed him and he wanted you gone. We were told to wait for you,' he said. 'And we each got a hundred dollars for doing the job.'

'For killing me, you mean.'

Buckley swallowed. 'Yeah. For . . . killing you. But like I said, I didn't want to do it, Steve. I swear.'

'Pete Taylor . . . ' said Karner, his voice trailing off. 'He still around Stayton?'

'He moved up to Seattle,' Buckley said. 'His little brother's still around, though.'

'Good,' Karner said, his face thoughtful.

'Pete put it all together. He's the feller you want to see,' Buckley said. 'We were just doing what we were told. He said they'd burn us out of our houses if we refused. It was all Pete.'

'You're quite helpful, ain't you?' Karner said, his voice laced with contempt. 'Yep. Mighty helpful.'

'I never felt right about what happened,' Buckley explained.

His mind raced as he tried to determine what Karner would do next. Would he kill him? Let him go? Turn him over to the police? The uncertainty was agonizing.

'Had a lot of sleepless nights over it,

Jack?' Karner asked.

'I guess I don't blame you if you don't believe me.'

'That's right,' Karner said, a smile tugging at the corners of his mouth. 'I don't believe you.' He sighed heavily and took another puff on his cigar. 'But I'm much obliged that you gave me Pete Taylor's name. Matter of fact, I'm so grateful that I've decided I'm going to give you a choice.'

Buckley's scalp tightened. He didn't know whether to be hopeful or scared.

'A choice?' he asked. 'What kind of a choice?'

Karner took a final pull on his cigar and flicked it past Buckley's shoulder into the canyon. He blew the smoke directly into Buckley's face.

'Only one of us is getting off this train in Salem,' he explained in a clipped tone. 'And that person ain't going to be you. But I'm going to do for you what you never did for me, that night you tried to kill me. I'm going to give you a fighting chance to live.'

The color had drained from Jack Buckley's face. Its characteristic smugness was gone now.

'What's this chance you're going to give me?' he asked, an element of desperation in his voice.

'Well, it's simple, really,' Karner said. 'I can either shoot you where you stand, or you can jump.'

Buckley laughed nervously. 'You're kidding, ain't you?'

There wasn't the slightest trace of humor in Steve Karner's face.

'I've never been more serious in my life, Jack.' He removed the big Navy Colt from the holster on his right hip and pointed it at Buckley's chest. 'Enough talking. It's time to make your choice, sidewinder.'

'You wouldn't shoot an unarmed man, Karner.' Buckley's statement was more of a plea than anything else.

'You sure about that?' Karner asked, pulling back the hammer on his Colt. 'After what you and those boys did to me?'

'Like I said, Steve — they made us do it. OK, they made *me* do it. Some of the boys hated your guts and were happy to help. But I — '

Karner's eyes were like chips of ice.

'Shut the hell up,' he said. 'I'm going to count to five. You either go over that rail alive, or I put a bullet through your head and send you over the rail dead. What's it going to be?'

'Steve — '

'One.'

'Please!'

'Two.'

Buckley pounded his hand against the carriage door, hoping to arouse attention. The old couple were still the only people inside, and they didn't respond to the noise.

'Three.'

Buckley shrieked, 'Goddamn it!'

'Four.'

Without another word, Jack Buckley pivoted to the rail and leapt over it, his hysterical screams echoing up the canyon walls as he plummeted downward. Karner stepped forward and watched the man fall.

There weren't any trees to break Buckley's descent. He fell sixty feet, twirling like a ragdoll in a tornado, before he slammed into a large rock protrusion that jutted out from the canyon wall. Blood exploded from his head on impact, silencing his terrified screams, and he bounced off the rock and continued to fall, disappearing finally into the shadows at the bottom of the canyon.

2

Steve Karner had been dead for three years.

The murder had taken place in a dense thicket of trees alongside the Santiam River, a couple miles east of Stayton, Oregon. It was July 1884. Karner was employed at the Lockhart Lumber Mill, working hard and earning good wages. He had been courting Patsy McCurtin for over a year, and it looked like they would soon be married.

It was a note about Patsy that brought Karner to the riverbank that night. One of the boys from the mill tapped on the door to the small cabin that Karner shared with his uncle on the outskirts of town. It was after eleven o'clock, and the summer sky was dark. The boy delivered the note and left. The note wasn't in Patsy's handwriting, but it asked for an urgent meeting; had it not sounded serious, Karner would never have saddled his horse and ridden out of town. It asked him to meet her at a local swimming hole. She would be there at quarter to midnight, waiting for him. Why she wanted to meet was unclear, but Karner knew she had to be in trouble to make a request like that. So he went.

The men were in the shadows, waiting for him to arrive. There were five of them, and he knew them all. They waited until he had dismounted and tied his sorrel to a sapling before they struck. The first blow had been delivered to the back of Karner's skull with a large river rock. He was nearly unconscious when he turned around and saw the faces of his attackers. They were all men who worked with him at the mill. They fell upon him before he had the chance to ask them the reason for the attack. They used logs, rocks, and their fists to pound him into unconsciousness, and then they bound his hands behind his back and threw him into the river. He was floating face-down on the rippling water when he disappeared around a bend. He had never been seen again.

Now it was early November 1887. The question of what had happened to him was now only rarely discussed. Most believed he had somehow fallen into the river and drowned; those with wilder imaginations claimed he had joined an outlaw gang and headed east to Montana. The general consensus, however, was that he was dead.

But Steve Karner was very much alive.

★   ★   ★

The night was drizzly and pitch dark as the two men made their way through the forest trail. They were both drunk, having spent much of their weekly wages from the Lockhart mill on whiskey and beer at one of Stayton's three saloons. This was their regular routine for Friday nights.

The bigger of the two men was named Gil Thompson. He was a strapping man, nearly five inches taller than six feet, with dark features and a few days of stubble on his jutting jaw. The smaller man was Clarence Snow. He was portly, with a florid face and a carefully groomed mustache. Thompson and Snow had been best friends since their first day together at the local schoolhouse. Two decades had passed, but they remained inseparable, sharing a cabin in the woods not far from the banks of the Santiam.

Although Snow was almost a foot shorter than Thompson, he had always been the dominant figure in their friendship. He was the one who had gotten Thompson a job at the mill; before that, the big man had labored in the forests, felling trees at logging camps and hating every minute of it. Operating a saw at the mill was a much more agreeable way of life, in Thompson's view. Snow agreed.

They were only a few hundred yards from their cabin, riding slowly down an incline, when they saw the man in the middle of the trail, sitting atop a large chestnut mare. The man had a cigar in his mouth and made no move to make way for the two men. He just sat there, blocking the trail. In the darkness, it was nigh impossible to make out the man's features.

Thompson and Snow pulled reins about fifteen feet from the man. They regarded him curiously. As he invariably did, Snow took the initiative.

'Hey there, feller,' he said. 'You want to move off the trail so me and my pard can pass?'

His words were reasonable enough, but there was an undercurrent of threat to his tone.

'Not particularly,' said the stranger, releasing a massive plume of smoke.

Thomson and Snow exchanged incredulous glances.

'Maybe you didn't hear what he said,' Thompson interjected.

21

'I heard just fine, Gil.'

Thompson slitted his eyes. 'How you know my name?' he asked.

'We're old friends,' the man said. He flicked his cigar into the trees. 'Ain't that right, Clarence?'

Snow leaned forward in the saddle. 'What's your name?' he demanded.

'I'm kind of hurt that you both forgot about me so soon.'

'Quit talking in circles,' Snow said, his patience at an end. He felt a strange uneasiness taking hold of him. 'If you're not going to say who you are, then get the hell off the trail so we can pass. We got to get up early.'

The stranger laughed. 'I already said I ain't moving, boys.'

Again Thompson and Snow exchanged glances.

'Is this some kind of joke?' Thompson asked, struggling to make sense of the conversation.

'No. It's no joke.'

'Say . . . ' remarked Snow, staring hard at the stranger. His insides turned cold. 'You look like — '

'Steve Karner.' The man's voice was loud and clear.

'You're lying!' Thompson shouted.

'No, I'm not,' Karner said calmly. 'I'm back from the dead, Gil. I came all the way from the other side to see you again.' He swept his eyes to Snow. 'And you, too, Clarence.'

The silence that followed was tense. Snow and Thompson were considerably more sober than they had been only a minute before.

'All right, then,' Snow said, trying to ease his nerves by talking. 'What do you want?' From where he sat, he could see the Navy Colt on Karner's hip. He wondered if he could get his pistol out of the holster before Karner did. Perhaps if Thompson distracted him . . .

'Can't a man just catch up on old times with two friends?' Karner asked.

'I know what you're thinking, Steve,' said Snow. 'You blame us for what happened.'

'You mean, for killing me?'

'Yes, damn it — that's what I mean. You have to remember that we were — '

'Only doing what you were told?'

Snow closed his mouth. He had never liked Steve Karner, and he hadn't shed a single tear for what he had helped do to him. He couldn't quite believe that Karner was here now, alive, talking to him. But if Karner was trying to frighten Clarence Snow, it wasn't going to work. Not with two men against one.

'Now, I'm done with this. I know you don't want to talk. What do you want?'

Karner was quiet for a moment, gazing at the two riders. Snow thought that Karner was looking through him rather than at him, and the hairs on the back of his neck stood up.

'What I want is to return the favor,' Karner said at last.

'What's that supposed to mean?' asked Thompson.

'It means I'm going to kill you both.'

The night air seemed suffused with danger. Snow and Thompson looked at each other, and Snow smirked. Then in a moment of panic, Thompson reached for his pistol. He had barely cleared leather when Karner's right hand streaked toward his hip. He palmed the Navy Colt, raised it, and fired one shot, hitting Thompson in the throat. The bullet blasted out of the back of the man's neck, and he dropped his pistol onto the ground, clawing at his throat. Blood oozed between his fingers and over his hands. A moment later, he slumped and tumbled sideways out of the saddle into the wet leaves on the ground.

Snow sat, mouth agape, watching. Raw terror gripped him and he began to babble, pleading with Karner. Tears streaked down his face as he begged for his life.

'It wasn't us, Steve. It was Pete Taylor! He made us do it! He wanted to marry Patsy and — '

'What did you say?' Karner asked thinly.

'It was Pete!'

'No, I mean about Patsy.'

Snow hesitated. 'Pete wanted to marry Patsy. It's why he paid us to kill you.'

Karner said nothing. He sat in the saddle, regarding Clarence Snow with no emotion, his face inscrutable.

'Please, Steve. Let me go. They said we'd lose our jobs and they'd burn us out of our cabins if we didn't go along with it.'

'Draw,' Karner said, sliding his Colt back in its holster.

'Wh-what?'

'You heard me. Draw.'

Snow blinked, his mind casting around for a way out of the situation in which he found himself. There was none, and he knew it. His hand shook as he reached down as fast as he could, dragging his pistol from the holster and, to his surprise, raising it and leveling it at Steve Karner. He was just about to squeeze the trigger when Karner moved. His hand was like a blur, and he was pointing his gun at Snow even as the latter prepared to fire.

'Rot in hell, Clarence,' Karner said, and then he fired a shot. It took Snow dead center in the forehead, hurling the man off his horse into the brush beside the trail. Both of the dead men's horses ran into the trees, vanishing in the night.

Karner replaced his weapon and touched spurs to his horse's flanks. He didn't bother to take a second look at the bodies on the ground.

⋆ ⋆ ⋆

Twenty minutes later, Karner stood in the shadows on the edge of a clearing, his horse tied to a tree nearby.

Powerful emotions stirred within him as he regarded the cabin in the middle of the clearing. He could see light behind the closed shutters and he knew Ash was home. This was the place where Karner had grown up, raised by his uncle from the age of two. By that time, both Karner's mother and father were dead.

Memories flooded his mind. Ash Karner was an easy-going man who had treated his nephew like the son he had never had. He was the older brother of Steve's father, and he had been devastated by the early deaths of his brother and sister-in-law. Despite his private pain, he had taken to fatherhood like a duck to water. He didn't have the temperament of a firm disciplinarian, so he had been relieved when the boy had shown that he didn't need to be disciplined very often. He had tried to be a good example by working hard, drinking and smoking in moderation, and taking his nephew to church once or twice a year. He had taught young Steve how to swim and ride a horse. Later he taught him to fish, and they had passed many happy hours fishing the Santiam.

Ash Karner had also taught him how to shoot. Ash was good with a gun, whether a pistol or a rifle, but even he had to acknowledge that his nephew was a natural. He would practice shooting at tin cans in the yard for hours on end, refining his already formidable inherent skill with guns. It was said he could outdraw anyone in Marion County. At ten years old, Steve Karner was making shots that stunned grown men. That year he won a shooting contest in Stayton that gave him a reputation throughout the Willamette Valley.

Ash was proud of that.

Those years were long behind him as Karner stood in the darkness, watching the cabin. He hadn't seen his uncle in three years and wondered how the old man would react when he saw his nephew.

Karner strode across the yard to the back door. He stood for a few moments there near the woodpile, scanning the trees around the edge of the clearing. When he was sure no one had followed him, he tapped on the door. He could hear movements inside the small house, and then his uncle's voice came to him through the door.

'Who is it?' asked Ash.

Karner grinned. The voice sounded exactly the same.

'An old friend,' he responded.

He could hear the bar being lifted inside, and then the door opened a couple of inches. Light spilled out onto Steve Karner, who removed his hat so his uncle could see him better. A squinting eye appeared in the crack in the doorway. The eye widened when Ash realized who was standing outside.

'Lord Almighty,' Ash said, pulling the door further open. 'It can't be.'

Tears welled in the old man's eyes. Steve Karner smiled, a lump forming in his throat.

'It's me, Ash,' he said. 'Can I come in?'

Ash moved aside to make room for Karner, who stepped into the warm cabin.

'Hell, yes, you can!' he said. 'Hell, yes!' He closed the door and clasped his hands to Karner's shoulders. 'Little Steve. I thought you were dead.'

'I know.'

'What happened? Where have you been?'

Karner sighed. 'I'll tell you everything, Ash. We've got a lot of catching up to do.'

He looked around the cabin and a warm feeling came over him. Nothing had changed.

'You want a shot of bourbon?' Ash asked, lifting a bottle from a shelf near the pot-bellied stove.

'I would indeed,' Karner said. He looked at his uncle and saw that, although his appearance was largely unchanged, he had a stoop now, and there was a sadness in his eyes that hadn't been there before.

Ash Karner filled two shot glasses and passed one to his nephew. The older man tossed the liquor back while the younger man took only a sip.

'Come on now — have a seat,' Ash said, pointing to a chair.

Karner sat down wearily and took another sip of the whiskey. 'It's good to be back,' he said. 'You look like you've been doing well.'

'We can talk about me later — tell me where you've been!'

'I've been in Idaho, mostly,' Karner explained.

'What happened? You went out one night and never came back. Word had it you hit your head and drowned in the river. I rode along the banks every day for months. I thought maybe I'd find your body.'

'I didn't hit my head,' Karner said slowly. 'Jack Buckley did. Along with Clarence Snow, Gil Thompson, Norm Ballard, and Dave Villiers. They hit me with clubs and rocks. They pistol-whipped me. Kicked me until I was out cold. Then they tied my hands behind my back and threw me into the river, good as dead. I don't know how I didn't drown, but I didn't. Came to on the riverbank near Salem. Spent two days just lying there, not even knowing who I was.'

His uncle's face was ashen as he

listened to Karner's words.

'Why, Steve? Why would they do it?'

'That's what I'm here to find out.'

'Why didn't you come back sooner?'

'I thought they'd kill me. I was in no shape to fight them, not for a long time. An old lady found me by the river and took me to where she and her husband lived in a little rundown shack. They didn't know who I was, but they took me in, tended to me until I almost felt human again. I was getting ready to come back here — and then the old feller brought a newspaper back from Salem. That's when I read about Patsy.'

Ash lowered his eyes and looked at the floor, shaking his head sorrowfully. 'A damn shame. She died six days after you disappeared. She was riding the riverbank, too, just like I was. Looking for you. Somehow her horse got spooked and she got thrown. She never woke up again.'

'I saw her obituary in the paper,' Karner continued, his face grim. 'I almost couldn't believe it. After that, I didn't want to come back. I hit the trail and went as far away from Stayton as I could get. For a while there, I didn't think I would ever come home again. But then I knew it was time. And here I am.'

'I'm so glad to see you, boy. You don't even know . . . '

'Same here, Ash,' Karner said, and put a hand on his uncle's shoulder. 'Same here.'

The happiness he felt at being home again was tempered by a smoldering anger at the men who had taken him away from here, who had tried to take his life, and who, he now knew, had caused the death of the woman he loved. Patsy McCurtin was killed while out searching for him. The only reason she was out there was because of the devious actions of those five cowardly killers. Now there were only two left.

Ash Karner seemed to be reading his nephew's thoughts.

'What are you going to do now, Steve?' he asked.

Karner raised his head. 'I'm going to kill every damn one of them,' he said. 'And I'm going to kill the man responsible for hiring them.'

'Hiring them?'

'Yes. They were told to kill me. Their jobs were threatened and they were told they'd be burned out of their homes if they didn't carry out the orders. Then they were each given a hundred dollars — a whole month's wages, just for killing a man they'd known their whole lives. Pete Taylor set the whole thing up. Probably not one of them lost a wink of sleep over what they did to me, or over what happened to Patsy. Well, they're going to pay for that. God help me — they will.' He polished off the rest of the bourbon. 'As a matter of fact, three of them already have.'

Ash's bushy white eyebrows shot up. 'What do you mean?'

'Jack Buckley's dead.'

'He is?'

'Yep. I was in Bend, waiting for the train to Salem. I spotted him on the platform, laughing and joking with his brother. He must have been visiting him. I almost couldn't believe it when I saw him. Jack Buckley — the biggest coward of them all, standing right there, no more than thirty feet away. He didn't spot me, or if he did, he didn't recognize me, now that I've grown this beard. I got on the train and bided my time. He went out on the platform to smoke, so I decided to join him. A minute later he went over the rail into a canyon. I gave him the chance to fly, but he just couldn't do it.'

'He always was a son of a bitch,' Ash confirmed. 'I don't think even his mother will miss him.' He scrubbed a hand across his face, considering his nephew's words. 'You said three were dead.'

Karner nodded. 'Clarence Snow and Gil Thompson are no longer with us. I reckon someone will find their bodies tomorrow. I gave them each a fair chance to shoot me. They were a little slower on the draw than I was.'

'Good Lord, boy. Don't go off and get yourself hanged.'

'I don't intend to, Ash. Nobody knows I'm back. Hell, nobody knows I'm even alive. I'm going to keep it that way until I get my pound of flesh. Then I'm going after Pete Taylor.'

Ash rose and refilled his glass. Karner accepted a refill, too.

'Pete's not around here anymore,' Ash said. 'He moved up north somewhere.'

'That's what I heard. I'm going to find some way to get him to come back. Then I'm going to kill him. When that's done, maybe I can start to live my life again. I won't be free until I make every damn one of them pay for what they did. Not just to me, but to Patsy, too.'

'I understand your desire for revenge, Steve. I really do. But you better be careful — real careful. You could get yourself killed.'

'I know it. Believe me, Ash — I'm going to be careful. I've been planning this a long time now. I'm not going to do anything hasty that might get me caught, or killed. But this has to be done. That's all there is to it.'

Ash nodded gravely. His face was pensive as he gazed at the nephew he thought he would never see again, and whose disappearance and apparent death had caused him so much grief. He had experienced countless sleepless nights over it. He had even turned to drinking, and although it never got out of hand, he was consuming more liquor than he ever had before. Sometimes it was the only way he could sleep at night, or get through the day. But now Steve was back, sitting right here in the cabin with him. The whole turn of events was almost too much for the old man to take in.

'What do you need from me?' he asked. 'I'll do anything I can to help you.'

'Thanks, Ash. I'm just going to need a place to stay.'

'Well, here it is. This is your home as much as it is mine.'

'I knew I could count on you. Good old Ash.'

'Family is family. That's all there is to it.'

'I know. I'm sorry to drag you into the middle of this, but if everything goes the way I planned, you won't have any problems on my account.'

'I ain't worried about any problems, boy. I'm just glad to have you back.'

3

A few hours later, Steve Karner fell into a deep slumber on the plank floor of his childhood home. It had been years since he had slept as well as he did that night. Ash had tried to get the younger man to take the bed, but Karner wouldn't hear of it. When Karner awakened the next morning, he felt thoroughly refreshed. It was, indeed, good to be home.

He passed the day helping Ash take care of things around the property. The small homestead was located in an isolated area just outside of town; it had, Ash noted, been years since anyone had ridden out to see him. Karner wasn't worried about being discovered. He helped his uncle repair a fence, then did some work on the roof of the small barn. He was up on the barn, hammering in some shingles, when Ash brought his old sorrel out of the stable and announced that he was riding into town to get some food.

'I'll be back in a couple hours,' he said. 'You need anything while I'm there?'

Karner thought about it for a moment, and then shook his head.

'I've got everything I need,' he said.

'I'll let you know if I hear anything in town.'

'I would be surprised if someone hasn't found Thompson and Snow by now,' Karner observed. 'I didn't make any attempt to hide them.'

'Those two bushwhackers deserved what they got,' Ash said.

'I don't think anyone will ever find Jack Buckley. Or what's left of him — and I don't think that's much.'

'Suits me fine,' Ash said indifferently. He exhaled heavily. 'All right then. Keep your pistol handy.'

'I will.'

Ash neck-reined his mount and heeled it toward the trail in the woods that led to the main road into town. He vanished into the trees and Karner went back to repairing the roof.

★   ★   ★

Ash alighted in front of the general store and tied his reins to the hitching post. It was a busy morning in Stayton. The boardwalks were bustling with activity, and there was a large crowd on the steps in front of the store.

Ash climbed the steps and went inside. Ed Cook, the owner of the store, was standing near the front window, watching the people outside.

'Morning, Ash,' he said distractedly.

'Morning, Ed. What's all the ruckus about?'

'You haven't heard?'

'No, I don't guess I have. Heard what?'

'They found Clarence Snow and Gil Thompson this morning. They'd been shot dead right near their cabin.'

Ash's face showed surprise. 'I'll be

damned,' he said. 'They have any idea who did it?'

Cook spread his hands. 'No idea at all. The marshal's looking into it. He got a buckboard and brought their bodies into town.'

'Sounds like they messed with the wrong person,' Ash said.

'That wouldn't surprise me a bit,' Cook agreed. 'They never really liked anyone but each other. And they could never keep their mouths shut.'

'I know I never had any use for them.'

Cook turned and looked at Ash. 'You looking for something in particular today?'

'Thought I might buy a ham and some beans. Maybe some fruit if you have any in tins.'

'I sure do,' Cook said, leading Ash over to the shelves where the tinned goods were kept.

Fifteen minutes later, Ash exited the store. The crowd out front had begun to disperse. He stood there for a

43

moment, listening to the conservation of the stragglers.

'Another strange thing,' one man said. 'I heard nobody's seen Jack Buckley for two days. He ain't shown up at the mill and there ain't no sign of him at his place. He's never missed a day of work in his life.'

One of the other men said, 'Hell, maybe it was Jack who killed Gil and Clarence.'

Ash smiled to himself and put his items in his saddlebags. He untied the reins and mounted, turning down Main Street in the direction of his homestead. He halted when he saw Marshal Ethan Bursofsky coming up the street on his horse, a worried expression on his face.

Bursofsky was in his early forties. He had lived in Stayton all his life, serving as marshal for more than a decade. He was scrupulous about his work, treating all the residents of his town with equal impartiality. This had at times caused difficulties for him, particularly when powerful families like the Lockharts expected special treatment. It was a testament to the marshal's integrity that he had stayed in office for as long as he had, and that he retained the support of the great majority of local residents.

Ash Karner respected him more than any other lawman he had known in many decades in Stayton — and he had seen his fair share of marshals come and go. He nodded in greeting at the marshal when the latter pulled up beside him.

'I heard about Gil and Clarence, Marshal,' Ash said. 'Who found them?'

'John Evans,' Bursofsky said. 'He found their horses in a field about a mile from their spread.'

'No idea about who might have done it?' Ash tried to put a concerned expression on his face, and partially succeeded.

'Not one,' Bursofsky said pensively. 'Damnedest thing I've seen in years. Both of them still had money in their pockets, too. Whoever shot them wasn't interested in robbing them, that's for sure. It seems more like some kind of personal grudge, I reckon.'

'Who you figure would have a grudge like that against them two?'

'I don't know. They weren't the friendly sort, but I can't think of anyone who'd want to kill them in cold blood.'

'The world's a crazy place,' Ash said in a sagacious tone. He sighed. 'Anyway, I better get on home. You take care, Ethan.'

'Will do.' Bursofsky spurred his horse toward the marshal's office at the end of the block. Ash gave him one last look before beginning the trek home.

When he rode into his yard, Ash saw that his nephew had completed the repairs to the barn roof. Karner was standing at the well, filling a bucket with water. He waved at Ash when he heard him approach.

'Any news?' he asked.

'They found them both,' Ash said, stepping down from the saddle. 'You should have emptied their pockets before you left them. I could have bought another ham.'

Karner laughed. 'I ain't a thief.'

Ash made a dismissive gesture. 'I was just kidding. Nobody in town has the slightest idea of who might want to kill those gents.' He opened one of his saddle bags and took out some tins of food. 'Oh — and I heard a feller discussing Jack Buckley, too.'

'Yeah?'

'He was saying it was mighty peculiar that nobody's seen Jack for a few days. Said he never missed work before now.'

'He's going be missing a lot more work,' said Karner, hefting the bucket and following Ash into the cabin. 'He'll be missing work forever, in fact.'

When Ash went back out and fetched the ham from his other saddlebag, Karner used the water to boil some coffee. Ash got out a big cast iron pot and began assembling their dinner. Finally, he sat down at the table and sipped at his coffee.

'You look like you got something on your mind, Ash,' Karner said.

47

Ash looked into his coffee cup for a moment before speaking.

'You know I support what you're trying to do here, boy,' he said. 'I think the bastards who did this, and who helped cause Patsy's death, deserve everything that's coming their way. But talking with the marshal this morning made me think.'

'About what?' Karner asked.

'Well, you're playing for big stakes here. Mighty big stakes. If you slip up and get caught, Bursofsky won't have any choice but to hang you, even if he understands why you did what you done.'

'I understand that.'

'I know he wouldn't want to do that. And I sure as hell wouldn't want to see that.' Ash took another drink of his coffee and swirled it around in his tin cup. 'All I'm saying is that I hope you'll be real careful. I think with Clarence, Gil, and Jack all missing or dead, the other fellers who were involved with this are going to be on guard. They might put the pieces together and set a trap for you.'

Karner grinned reassuringly. 'I appreciate your concern, Ash. I do. Let me tell you, I've been thinking this over for a long spell. I'm going to take my time. I hope they are sweating now, the other sons of bitches who did this. They can try to set a trap, but it won't work.'

'What's your plan?'

'Ballard and Villiers are next. I ain't in a rush. I'm going to do a little scouting tonight after dark. They both still live where they did before?'

'Yes, they do.'

'Good. I'll head out tonight and take a look at things. Finding Buckley the way I did was pure luck. Gil and Clarence lived out in the middle of nowhere, so I wasn't worried about anyone coming along and spoiling the festivities. I'm going to have to be a bit more stealthy when I go for Ballard and Villiers. If the time ain't right this evening, then I'll wait.'

'What about Pete Taylor?'

'I'm saving him for last. Me and him are going have a little talk. Clarence said Pete put them up to do this because he wanted to marry Patsy himself.'

Ash was incredulous. 'Pete and Patsy? I never heard of such a thing.'

'That's what I thought, too. But somehow he's behind this. I don't know why, but I'm going to learn everything I want to know before I'm through with him.'

Ash set his coffee cup on the table and sat back in his chair. 'As long as you've thought this through, Steve,' he said. 'You're only going to get one shot to take care of this business.'

Karner's grin was still in place, but there was no humor in his eyes.

'That's all I'm going to need.'

4

Norm Ballard lived with his wife on a quiet dirt road about a half-mile from the Lockhart mill. There were five other houses on the road, which was bordered on one side by the river and on the other by the forest.

Steve Karner had picketed his horse among the trees and stood behind a large maple at the rear of the Ballards' back yard. He was sure he hadn't been observed as he rode through the forested outskirts of Stayton. It was just after two o'clock in the morning as he lurked in the shadows, watching the house for any kind of activity. He saw none.

He tied a bandana around his face and waited for a few minutes more before he stepped out from behind the tree. He was just about to make his way across the dewy grass to the back door when sounds from inside the house halted him. He quickly moved back behind the tree, his senses keen.

Karner's breathing was shallow as he watched the back door open from the inside. A moment later, Norm Ballard emerged, wearing his long johns, over which he had pulled a pair of pants that he was buttoning as he stepped into the yard.

He hasn't changed a bit, Karner thought. Same big, dumb lummox he always was.

Ballard was a large man in his mid-twenties. He was prematurely bald and exceptionally strong. Like the other men who had attacked Karner, Ballard worked at the Lockhart mill. He was a stupid man with the temperament of a bully. He had seemed to take much pleasure in the beating he administered the night Karner was almost killed, and Steve Karner hadn't forgotten that.

Karner's eyes tracked Ballard as the man turned to the left and walked to the outhouse. He went in and slammed the door behind him.

Karner moved swiftly, crossing the yard and stopping near a tree about five feet from the outhouse. He stood there in silence, waiting. A minute later, the out-house door opened and Ballard stepped out.

Karner had a large buck knife in his right hand. He used his left arm to encircle Ballard's neck, squeezing tightly to keep the man from yelling, and pulled him back toward the trees at the edge of the yard.

Ballard's eyes bulged and he attempted to cry out. His strong hands reached up and gripped Karner's arm, trying to pry it away from his neck. Karner raised the knife and held in front of Ballard's face. Moonlight glinted off the huge blade.

'Hello there, Norm,' Karner said, his mouth close to Ballard's ear. 'It's your old friend, Steve. Remember me?'

Ballard kept staring at the knife. Sweat covered him despite the coldness of the night air. Karner released the pressure on the man's neck.

'You — ' Ballard muttered in a

strangled voice. 'How?'

'It's a miracle,' Karner said. 'The Lord brought me back from the dead to settle a few scores.'

'Clarence and Gil,' Ballard said hesitantly.

'Yeah, I settled those scores. Jack Buckley, too.'

'It wasn't my idea, Steve.'

'Of course not.'

'You got to believe me!'

'Who was it?' Karner said. 'Who told you to do it?'

He wanted to see if Ballard's story would be any different from the story told by Buckley, Snow, and Thompson.

'Pete Taylor.'

'Why?' He brought the knife closer to Ballard's face. 'Why would Pete Taylor want to have me killed?'

'He didn't really say,' Ballard insisted. 'Something to do with Patsy.'

'And you went along with it. I seem to recall you were having yourself a real good time that night, hitting me over the head.'

Ballard tensed. 'I was drunk as hell,' he said. 'I barely remember it.'

'I remember it,' Karner said, his face set in harsh lines. He tightened his arm around Ballard's neck. 'I remember it real good.'

Suddenly Ballard made his move. He could tell from Karner's words that this was no social call; the fates of his dead friends only confirmed it, although he hadn't linked their deaths to Karner until now. His only chance was to kill Karner before the latter killed him.

He brought his elbow hard into Karner's ribcage. Although they were roughly equal in size, Ballard had a primal strength that made him a formidable fighter. Karner grunted and the pressure on Ballard's neck lessened just enough for him pull free. He turned and faced Karner, grabbing his wrist and twisting until the buck knife fell into the grass.

'You made a mistake,' Ballard said with a wicked gleam in his eye. 'You should have just killed me instead of flapping your jaws.'

They circled each other, both wary. The bandana had slipped from Karner's face down to his neck. Karner moved toward the knife, but Ballard stepped in quickly and reached down to pick it up. Karner kicked him hard in the side of the head, sending the big man sprawling. With a speed that was remarkable for a man of his size, Ballard leapt back to his feet and charged, smashing his shoulder into Karner's chest. They fell together onto the ground, wrestling momentarily.

Ballard wrapped his thick fingers around Karner's throat and tightened his grip, digging his thumbs in to cut off the air. Karner's vision darkened and he blinked, trying to stay conscious. He slammed his fists into Ballard's face, repeating the process a few more times, but the blows were ineffectual. Ballard could take a punch, and he knew Karner was in trouble.

Karner scraped his nails down Ballard's face, slicing the flesh and leaving bloody marks, Ballard gasped, but still his claw-like fingers encircled Karner's throat. Karner punched him again, with all the strength he could muster, but it had no effect on Ballard's grip. Through his dimming vision he could see Ballard's eyes. They were glowing with determination and blood-lust.

Karner thrust his finger into Ballard's left eye, feeling the squishiness of the eyeball as it gave under the pressure. Ballard emitted an anguished cry and instantly released Karner, who rolled over onto his back, sucking in lungfuls of air. Ballard was rolling in the grass, clutching his eye.

'You son of a bitch!' he said.

Karner pushed himself to his feet and stumbled toward the knife. He leaned over and grasped the handle, but Ballard wasn't through yet. He was back on his feet, moving quickly toward Karner. Karner looked at Ballard's face and saw that the man's eye seemed to be a bloody orb in his head. Blood and pus oozed from between his swollen eyelids. Still he wanted to fight.

He took a swing at Karner and clipped him on the chin, forcing him off balance. Before Karner could respond, Ballard was on him, his face contorted with rage. He grasped Karner in a murderous bear hug and again they went down into the grass. Ballard landed on top of him, and at that moment he gasped, his body convulsing for a few seconds before becoming still. Karner lay there for several moments, his chest heaving, before he pushed Ballard off him. The handle of the buck knife protruded from Ballard's chest. It had entered just below the sternum, killing him almost instantly. Karner hadn't even been aware of the knife entering Ballard's body. In his eagerness to kill Karner, Ballard had inadvertently killed himself.

Karner sat up, resting his arms across his knees as he tried to regain his bearings. He was covered in blood — Norm Ballard's blood. The smell of it nearly made him retch, but he fought off the urge. He reached over and pulled the knife from Ballard's chest, wiping it off on the man's pants. Then he rose to his feet, his head still swimming from being choked.

He swept his eyes around the yard, worried that the fight had attracted attention. Nothing stirred in the early morning darkness. He turned and walked back into the trees toward where he had left his horse.

$\star$ $\star$ $\star$

It took Karner a half hour to reach the cemetery, which was located on a hill above Stayton. He had carefully skirted the town, riding through the woods when he could. His throat still throbbed from where Ballard had choked him, and there was a shooting pain there whenever he swallowed. The situation had come dangerously close to slipping out of Karner's control, but he put the thought out of his mind as he pulled leather near the gate of the cemetery. A thick fog lay over the graves, obscuring some of the tombstones. But Karner knew what he was looking for.

The McCurtin family plot was in a corner of the cemetery, near a thicket of maple trees. Karner alighted and led his horse through the fog to the line of tombstones there. He moved down to the end and, thumb-snapping a match, knelt to read the words on the newest stone: *Patsy McCurtin, Beloved Daughter and Sister, 1864–1884.* The wind rustled the leaves above him as he stared at the stone.

He had known Patsy since they were both little kids. Ash was a good friend to Patsy's father, and young Steve had attended school in the same one-room schoolhouse as Patsy, who was a few years behind him. He sometimes thought that he had been in love with her for as long as he could remember, and she had always returned the sentiment. Their bond had been intense from an early age.

His thoughts turned to Pete Taylor. Taylor's father owned hundreds of acres of forested land outside town, and he had made a fortune selling timber to the Lockharts. Along with his younger brother, Phil, Pete had been a schoolyard bully, tormenting the other kids with his fists and his sharp tongue. Only a few of his peers had been willing to stand up to Pete Taylor, and Steve Karner was one of them.

On one memorable occasion, Taylor had tripped a smaller boy in the yard, sending him sprawling into the dirt and nearly breaking the boy's spectacles. Before Taylor knew what was happening, Karner had grabbed him by the arm, turned him around, and hit him with all his might, bloodying his nose and knocking him into the dirt beside the boy Taylor had just struck. Taylor had leapt to his feet, and only the intervention of the teacher had prevented a full-blown fight from breaking out. Pete Taylor had never forgotten the incident, and for the rest of their childhoods, he had been a sworn enemy of Steve Karner. However, the animosity had seemed to diminish when they entered adulthood, although they had never been friends.

When Jack Buckley, Clarence Snow, Gil Thompson, and now Norm Ballard had all placed the blame on Pete Taylor, Karner had been surprised. Even more surprising was the idea that Taylor had masterminded the attack in order to pursue Patsy McCurtin. Never had Taylor shown even the slightest interest in Patsy; in fact, he had had a string of lovers until his parents had intervened to stop his impropriety. Although Karner couldn't completely reject the idea that Pete Taylor had been behind the attempt on his life, and that his motivation had been a secret longing for Patsy, there was something about the entire scenario that didn't ring true.

Whatever had compelled Taylor to organize the attempt on Karner's life, there could be no question that he was ultimately responsible for what had occurred. For Karner, that meant one thing: Pete Taylor was going to pay, and pay dearly.

Before that happened, though, Karner was going to make time for Dave Villiers.

Karner rose, still gazing at Patsy's tombstone, and removed his hat. All of his plans for the future, plans for marrying Patsy and settling down to start a family, plans for sharing his life with the woman he loved and had always loved, were gone now. The only thing that he could do now was to rectify the wrongs he had suffered, and which a group of men whom he had known his entire life had unleashed upon him one dark night on the river bank.

'You didn't deserve what happened, Patsy,' he said quietly. 'I would rather be dead than know that you were gone. But I promise you one thing — those who did this to us are going to wish they hadn't. Every single one.'

Only when he had tasted full retribution would Steve Karner be able to live again.

★ ★ ★

Karner got home not long before dawn. He saw a lantern burning in the cabin and knew that Ash was up, waiting for him.

He dismounted and put his horse in the stable, where he gave it oats and water. He brushed the animal before leaving it in the stall. When he came into the cabin, Ash was at the table, eating a biscuit and reading an almanac. He raised his head when he saw his nephew.

'I was getting worried, boy,' he said. He saw the red marks on Karner's throat where Ballard had attempted to strangle him — and nearly succeeded. 'Good Lord, Steven! What happened?'

Karner pulled out a chair and heaved himself into it. He removed his hat and tossed it onto the table.

'Norm Ballard damn near got the best of me,' he admitted. 'The man had fingers of iron.'

'Had?' Ash asked.

Karner nodded. 'He's dead, along with his other three pards.'

Ash took another bite from his biscuit and chewed it thoughtfully. Wood crackled in the stove.

'I'm damn glad you got the upper hand,' he said.

'He killed himself, really,' Karner noted. 'Jumped on me and knocked me to the ground when I had the buck knife in my hand. He fell right on top of it — took it all the way to the hilt.' He rubbed his neck, wincing with pain. 'He was long on muscle but short on brains.'

'He always was,' said Ash. 'A nasty piece of work since he was a kid. Never changed.'

'He said the same thing the others did — that Pete Taylor was behind all this.'

'Well, I guess there's no other way it could be,' Ash responded.

'I suppose. But it just doesn't make sense to me.'

'Me neither.' Ash finished his biscuit and brushed some crumbs from the front of his shirt.

'Maybe I'll be able to get some more information from Dave Villiers before he leaves this mortal coil,' Karner said. 'If not, it'll come down to Pete himself. He'll have some explaining to do, when we finally come face to face.'

5

Dave Villiers had been jumpy ever since the bodies of Clarence Snow and Gil Thompson had been found. With Jack Buckley's apparent disappearance, his discomfort had increased. But the killing of Norm Ballard had pushed him to the edge of psychological collapse.

Steve Karner was dead. Villiers knew that. The beating Karner had received on the riverbank that night had left him inches from death. When they tied his hands and threw his limp body into the river, it had to have killed him. It just had to.

Yet someone knew about the five men who killed Karner. There was no other explanation for the deaths and disappearance of four of the five attackers. And Dave Villiers knew what this meant — he was next.

It had only been three days since the murders started, but the strain was taking its toll on Villiers. His hands shook constantly and he had a headache that wouldn't go away. He tried to counter these things by drinking more, but it only made them worse, and for the last two mornings he had suffered from horrific hangovers. Still, he didn't know what else to do except continue drinking. It was the only thing that diverted his mind from what seemed to him to be impending doom.

Villiers wasn't a religious man, but the morning they found Norm Ballard's body, he had felt compelled to pull down the old family Bible from the shelf where he kept it, just above the stove in his small cabin. He hadn't bothered to go to the mill that morning. He had planned on going in, but when he heard about Norm he went instead to the general store and bought another bottle of bourbon, which he carried home and started on immediately. He was soon so drunk he could scarcely focus on the words in the Bible, which he had spread open on the rough wooden table. His hands were still shaking so badly that he spilled whiskey on the pages twice.

'Damn it!' he said, wiping the liquid off the page. It smeared the ink on the old Bible. Villiers thought of what his mother would say if she were still around. That Bible had meant the world to her.

Then another thought occurred to him. What would his mother have thought if she had known what he had done to Steve Karner all those years ago? His mother had been an upright woman, stern but loving. Would she have disowned her son? Supported his hanging for murder?

Tears dripped down his cheeks. He pressed his trembling fingers against his eyes, trying to calm himself. He decided to stop thinking about his mother.

He reached out and lifted the bottle to his lips, drinking deeply. The bottle was almost empty and late afternoon was approaching. He hadn't slept soundly for seventy-two hours, but a pleasant sleepy feeling was coming over him. Corking the bottle, he rose and walked to the door of his shack. He clutched his pistol in his right hand as he pulled the door open and looked out into the forest that surrounded his home. There was no one there, which relieved him. He had felt as if someone were watching him ever since this whole thing had started.

Villiers breathed in the fresh air, squinting his eyes against the rays of the sun. He went back in and closed the door behind him, then walked over to his grimy bed and collapsed onto it. He was careful to put his pistol on the small table beside the bed, within easy reach. He rolled over onto his back, covering his eyes with his arm. Within minutes, he had fallen into a deep sleep, snoring softly.

Hours passed before he opened his eyes again. It was pitch dark in the cabin. Villiers blinked a few times in the darkness. Night had fallen, and he was drenched in cold sweat. He pushed his fingers through his hair and they came away wet. For a moment he lay still, his mind wandering. Then the awful reality of his situation returned and a feeling of dread filled the pit of his stomach. He wished it had only been a bad dream, and that he could wake up from it like he had from his nap. But it was real, and no amount of wishful thinking was going to change that.

He needed whiskey. There was only a little left in the bottle, so he would have to ride into town to get some more. He wasn't going to pass the rest of this evening without some fire water to ease his mind. Then again, he feared riding into town after dark. Whoever was doing the killing might be out there in the woods, waiting for Villiers. Maybe he would take his rifle along instead of just his pistol. More firepower to defend himself with. Or maybe, damn it, he should just stay here, where it was safe.

No one could get him inside his own shack.

Why didn't I get another bottle in town this morning, he thought dejectedly. I'm a real dumb son of a bitch sometimes!

His head throbbed and he lay there for a minute longer, considering his options. He had to have that whiskey, trouble be damned. He swung his legs over the side of the bed and began to sit up.

Suddenly he heard the sound of a match igniting and light filled the inside of the tiny house. Someone was sitting at his table, and he watched the flame at the end of the match move a few inches and touch the wick of the candle he kept in a coffee mug on the table.

'Christ Almighty!' exclaimed Villiers as the bright light of the candle revealed the person at the table. It was a man, tall and strong, with a thick beard and flinty blue eyes that regarded Dave Villiers with cold hatred. He knew who it was, and there was no denying it. This was no dream.

'Steve Karner,' Villiers said in a tremulous voice.

He was so frightened he didn't even think to reach for the pistol, which was only about a foot and a half from his hand. The fact that Karner had a pistol pointed directly at Villiers's head also served as a powerful deterrent to any sudden moves on the latter's part.

'Dave, old buddy,' Karner said. 'How you been?'

Villiers gulped. 'Not so good.'

'That so?' Karner asked. His tone was menacing in its nonchalance. 'Gee, I'm real sorry to hear that.'

'Are you . . . ' Villiers had a hard time forming the words. 'Are you here to . . . kill me?'

'Yes,' Karner said plainly. 'I'm going to kill you.' He paused. 'But first I want you to tell me some things.'

Villiers felt a strange calmness come over him. It was as if being confronted by the thing he feared the most was preferable to living with the uncertainty and fear that had been consuming him for days now. He realized that his headache had gone away.

'What do you want to know?' he asked.

'How did you get involved in all this?' Karner asked.

'It was Jack Buckley. He came to me and said that he and Norm Ballard were going to play a little trick on you. He said they were going to knock you around a little because Pete Taylor thought you needed to be brought down a few notches.'

'And you thought that was a dandy idea?'

'I never had anything against you, Steve. I told Jack I didn't want to be a part of it, but he said I either went along with it or I would pay. He and Norm threw me up against the wall outside the mill and asked if I wanted my shack burned.' Villiers looked down at his hands, which were clenched together in his lap. 'What could I do?'

'You could have told me,' Karner retorted. 'That would have solved the

74

whole thing. I would have handled it from there, believe me.'

Karner thought back to that terrible night. He remembered that Villiers was less aggressive and less enthusiastic than the others. Still, the man had administered blows right along with them.

'Did you get paid for it?'

Villiers nodded. 'Yes. A hundred dollars. Spent the whole thing on whiskey to try to forget what I'd done.'

'Who paid you?'

'Jack Buckley gave me the money. He said it was from Pete Taylor.'

'Why would Pete Taylor want me dead?'

'I heard it had something to do with Patsy.'

'What — Pete wanted to marry her? Pete never showed the slightest interest in her. He liked whores.'

Villiers shrugged. 'I'm just telling you what I heard.'

'I guess I'll have to get the answers from Pete, then.'

'He ain't around anymore, you know.

He's somewhere up north.'

'I know. I don't care where he is, we're going to have a conversation. And he's going to pay for what he did.'

'I'm sorry, Steve. I never wanted to be a part of this. It's the worst thing I ever done in my life.'

Karner regarded him in silence. He figured there was some truth in the man's words. Perhaps Dave Villiers was a weakling who really did think he had no other option . . .

His thoughts dispersed immediately as Villiers dived toward the nearby table and grabbed his pistol. He raised it toward Karner.

'Go to hell!' he screamed, but even as he made a last attempt to save his own life he knew it was hopeless.

Karner's hand barely moved as he pulled back on the trigger of his Navy Colt. The bullet took Villiers in the temple. Villiers collapsed onto the dirt floor, the pistol falling from his fingers. A dark pool of blood began to spread around his head.

Karner rose and looked down at the body. Whatever Villiers's role in the entire affair had been, he had sealed his own fate.

'Thanks for making it easy for me, Dave,' Karner said.

He blew out the candle and left the shack, leaving the door open behind him.

★ ★ ★

Two days passed before anyone thought to look for Dave Villiers. His nearest neighbor was a half-mile away, so no one had heard the gunshot that killed him. His body was bloated and beginning to smell when one of his friends from the mill stopped by the shack. An hour later, Ethan Bursofsky stood over Villiers's body. His features were hardened as he regarded the dead man.

Lou Cameron, the manager of the Lockhart mill, stood a few feet behind the Marshal of Stayton. He had been as baffled as anyone by the string of murders and the disappearance that was thinning the ranks of his employees.

'What do you make of it, Marshal?' Cameron asked.

He was holding a handkerchief over his face to block out the smell of the decaying body. Bursofsky was, too.

'I can't make heads or tails of this,' the lawman admitted. He turned and gestured toward the door. Both men walked out into the yard.

'No one has still seen any sign of Jack Buckley,' Cameron observed.

'What if he's the one doing this?' Bursofsky ventured.

'Hell, I guess that's a possibility. But I don't rightly see why he would do that. These fellers were his pards.'

'Yeah, I know.' Bursofsky exhaled slowly. 'I ain't saying that it is Jack, but I have to entertain the idea, if you know what I mean.'

'Sure.'

Bursofsky removed his Stetson and patted it absently against the side of his leg.

'I think the same person is doing all

of this,' he said. 'I don't know who it is, or why he's picking these particular fellows to kill, but it must have something to do with the mill.'

Cameron's face had a startled expression. 'The mill?' he asked. 'What do you mean?'

'All these men work at Lockhart's. What if it's someone from the mill who's killing them? Is there anyone there you can think of who might be capable of this kind of thing?'

Cameron scratched beneath his chin, looking past the marshal. After a moment, he shook his head.

'I can't think of anyone, Marshal,' he said. 'We've got some rough characters working there, but that's just how it works in the lumber business. Lots of the fellers like to get rowdy and drunk. Some of them like to fight — '

'Like Jack Buckley,' Bursofsky said.

'Yeah, Jack is a scrapper,' Cameron agreed. 'Hell, so was Norm Ballard. Both those fellers had a mean streak.'

'Gil Thompson, too. Not exactly a

sweet-natured character.'

'No, he wasn't.'

They heard a wagon rattling up the road toward them. It was the old man who owned the livery in Stayton. He was going to take Villiers's body into town for burial. Bursofsky and Cameron watched the wagon come out of the trees and approach them.

They wrapped the body in a blanket and helped the stableman carry it out to the buckboard. As the wagon disappeared down the road, Cameron turned back to Bursofsky.

'What are you going to do next, Marshal?' he asked.

'I don't know that I can do much,' Bursofsky said. 'Maybe I'll deputize a few men to ride around and patrol at night.'

'That's a good idea.'

'The only other choice I have is to wait for the killer to strike again. And I think he will.'

6

Phil Taylor's house was a large two-storey structure. It was located in Stayton's most exclusive residential neighborhood. His neighbors included the mayor, both of the town's lawyers and its only judge, the doctor, and, at the end of the street, the Lockhart family, whose mansion was the largest house in town and one of the largest houses in the entire state of Oregon.

Taylor's father had built the house for his second son shortly before Phil's marriage to Amelia Lockhart, the youngest daughter of the town's most prominent citizen. The Taylors and the Lockharts had been closely associated for more than two decades, and what brought them together was the lumber industry. It had made both families very rich, although the Lockharts' fortune was substantially larger than that of the

Taylors. The relationship had been mutually beneficial, and so it made sense for the families to intermarry.

Apart from the servants who worked in the homes there, the street where Phil Taylor lived was rarely visited by the locals. That was the way Taylor and his neighbors liked it. It added to the feeling of exclusivity that they cherished.

The back yards of each of the homes on Water Street were bordered by the Santiam River. Taylor stood on the grass above the river, gazing down on the rippling water and smoking his pipe. He had his pistol in the holster on his hip, and a loaded shotgun leaned against a tree a few yards away. If the killer was going to come for him, Phil Taylor didn't plan on going down easily.

Every door and window in the house was locked. This was a new custom in the Taylor house, but Taylor had ordered the maid to see to it four days before, and he found himself double-checking every night before he went to bed. The only way someone would get into his house was by breaking a window or kicking in a door, which Taylor hoped would give him time to grab a gun and defend himself. Whoever was killing the men at the mill — the men who had been involved in murdering Steve Karner — wouldn't be able to slip into the house without being detected.

Taylor wasn't a paranoid man by nature, and he realized that the vengeance killer might not even be aware of his brother's involvement in the plot to kill Steve Karner. But Pete was no longer around, and if the killer did know of his involvement, Phil reckoned he might be the most convenient target.

He tapped out the dottle in his pipe against the side of a tree and then put the pipe in his pocket. He rubbed a hand down his face and silently cursed his brother for getting him into this situation. His own knowledge of the plot to kill Karner was murky. Pete had told him very little, and he had only shared the information with Phil because he was drunk. He had told him that someone had given him $5,000 to have Steve Karner killed. He said he had found three men to do it, and that two others had volunteered to help. He told Phil who the men were, but he refused to say who it was who had hired him to set the entire thing up.

It was gambling that had gotten Pete Taylor mixed up in the entire mess to begin with. Pete had been a compulsive gambler his entire adult life, to the point where his father had cut him off. Pete was always short of money, and always having trouble with the unsavory types he associated with in the gambling halls and saloons he frequented. His heavy drinking had only exacerbated his problems.

Phil Taylor sighed, cursing his brother under his breath. Pete was three years older, but he had always been the irresponsible one. Phil had been forced many times over the years to intervene on

Pete's behalf with their parents. It was as if Pete was a whirlpool, and he always found a way to pull Phil into it. This, though, was unlike any trouble Pete had been in before. And it threatened to harm Phil, or even get him killed, if his suspicions were correct.

It was thoroughly dark out now, with nary a star to be seen in the cloudless sky. The yard where Taylor stood ended at a steep embankment above the river. A thick tangle of large tree roots projected down into the water. Taylor's thoughts were interrupted by his wife's voice.

'Phil,' she called.

He turned and saw her standing on the back porch. She was silhouetted by lights inside the house.

'Yes, dear?' he said.

'Everything all right?'

He smiled. 'Everything's fine. I'll be in in a couple of minutes. Just wanted to take in some air.'

She returned his smile. 'Good. I was starting to get worried. If you want some of that pie, there's plenty left over from last night.'

'I'll be wanting some more — if you don't eat it all before I come in.'

She laughed and waved, then turned back into the house. He heard the door close behind her.

He breathed in the air, smelling the river. He could see her moving behind the curtains in the dining room. Then a sound caught his attention and he pivoted back toward the riverbank. He drew a sharp breath as he looked toward the water, not quite believing what he was seeing.

A dark shape was moving up the tree roots toward him. He narrowed his eyes and leaned forward, and suddenly the shape leapt up onto the bank and a wet hand gripped his throat as his mind struggled to comprehend what was happening to him. Taylor tried to scream, but the words wouldn't come, in part because of the fingers enclosed around his neck, and in part because of sheer, intense terror. A man had climbed out of the river and now held Phil Taylor in a vice-like grip. Taylor's hand moved down toward the pistol on his hip, but it was already too late . . .

★   ★   ★

Marshal Ethan Bursofsky was dead tired as he slid his foot into a stirrup and pulled himself up into his saddle in the circular driveway in front of Edward Lockhart's mansion.

He had hoped to get some insights into the murders of the mill workers, but the old man seemed as baffled by the crimes as the marshal himself was. He suggested that there was a madman loose in Stayton, murdering at random. Bursofsky wasn't convinced. When their meeting came to an end, Bursofsky paused in the foyer before heading out onto the marble steps in front of the house.

Coming down the stairs toward him was Tom Lockhart, one of the patriarch's twin sons. The young Lockhart grinned and waved toward the marshal. He was a small man, approaching thirty years old, with dark brown hair and spectacles. Unlike the Taylor boys, whose father was the second-richest man in the Stayton area, Lockhart wasn't known for putting on airs. If anything, he was one of the most widely liked men in town, with a quiet, friendly demeanor, and a reputation for fairness toward his employees at the Lockhart mill. This was in stark contrast to his twin brother, Paul, who was as surly and arrogant as Tom was easy going. Bursofsky saw no sign of Paul.

'Evening, Marshal,' Tom said genially. 'What brings you by?'

'I wanted to have a talk with your pa,' Bursofsky said.

'What about?'

'The killings that have been taking place.'

Tom Lockhart's face darkened. 'Yes, I've heard about them, of course. Everybody's talking about it. You got any idea what it's all about?'

Bursofsky spread his hands. 'Not a clue. I was hoping maybe your pa might know something, but he doesn't seem to have any ideas, either.'

'Well, Pa's not involved in the day-to-day running of the mill as much as he used to be, especially since his eyesight started going south. I've taken over most of that business for him.'

'You got any theory about why somebody might be killing your men?'

'Can't say I do, Marshal. I wish I could help. We've had to bring in men from Salem to fill their positions at the mill.' He frowned. 'You think there's some sort of connection to the mill — some reason this killer is choosing them?'

'I think that's likely. We have one missing man and four men murdered in less than a week. Every single one worked for your family's business. I've tried to wrap my mind around it, but I think it has to be linked to the mill.'

Lockhart crossed his arms, thinking over the marshal's words.

'If there's anything I can do to help, all you have to do is ask,' he said. 'If you want to come down tomorrow to talk to some of the men, you're more than welcome to do so. This is a terrible thing, these murders. I can't remember anything like it happening here in Stayton before.'

'Nor can I.'

'It's pretty frightening, that's for sure. But as I said, you can come on down to the mill and talk to anybody you please. I'll see to it.'

'I'm grateful, Tom. I think I just might take you up on that offer.'

Lockhart extended his hand and the marshal shook it firmly. 'Have a good evening.'

'Same to you,' Bursofsky said.

He went out through the door and down the steps to where his sorrel was tied to a lamp post on the side of the driveway. It was dark and brisk out. A sudden wind blew some dead leaves across the yard. Bursofsky buttoned up his coat and untied his horse. Seconds later he was riding off the Lockhart property and turning right up Water Street toward the center of town.

A woman's piercing shriek caused the marshal to pull leather and reach for his pistol. He looked to his right and realized he had halted in front of Phil and Amelia Taylor's house. When he heard another scream, he leapt from the saddle, tossing the reins over his horse's head. He moved across the yard to the side of the house and began creeping along the path toward the back of the property.

The Taylors' yard was meticulously maintained, with sculpted shrubbery and neatly trimmed rose bushes. Large trees cloaked the lawn in shadows, although light shone through the windows at the back, offering a little illumination.

Bursofsky came up to the left side of the back porch and halted, his eyes sweeping over the yard. Two men were struggling near the edge of the lawn, just above the river. One he recognized as Phil Taylor. The other man was shirtless and bootless, his hair and beard wet, his bare upper body glistening with water from the river. He was getting the better of Taylor, and Bursofsky saw him twist Taylor's arm away from the pistol on his hip. Taylor let out a cry of pain, and the shirtless man pulled the pistol from the young man's holster.

'Halt, there!' Bursofsky yelled, striding out past the edge of the porch. His pistol was raised and pointed at Taylor and the stranger. To his right, Bursofsky could see Amelia Taylor on the porch. She must have been the one whose screams he had heard from the street.

The shirtless man looked toward the marshal. His left hand still gripped Taylor's arm, and he released him, pushing him down onto the grass. The pistol in his other hand was pointed at Taylor.

'Drop that pistol, feller!' warned Bursofsky. He took a few more steps toward the man. 'I'm the town marshal, and I'll shoot you where you stand.' The man hesitated, looking back and forth between the lawman and the cringing man on the ground. Finally, he tossed his weapon aside. Relief washed over Ethan Bursofsky. 'Now you step away from Mr. Taylor and put your hands in the air.'

After a moment, the man complied. Taylor's wide eyes glinted in the light coming from the back of the house. He raised a trembling finger and extended it toward the man who had emerged from the river.

'Marshal,' he said in a warbling voice. 'Marshal — '

'What is it, Phil?' Bursofsky said. 'You know this feller?'

'It's Steve Karner!'

Bursofsky moved closer to the man with no shirt. 'Steve Karner?' he said incredulously. 'It can't be.'

'It's him!' Taylor exclaimed. He seemed almost hysterical.

Bursofsky kept his pistol on the stranger. 'You got a name, partner?'

'Yes, I do,' the man said, defiance in his face. 'I'm Steve Karner.' He smiled reluctantly. 'It's been a long time, Ethan.'

7

It was cold in the cell, so Bursofsky gave Karner an extra blanket. He also gave him a clean shirt he kept in a drawer in his desk in the front office. The cell was perfectly tidy, and Karner remembered that very few people ever ended up in the Stayton jail, apart from the occasional rowdy drunk.

Bursofsky had lighted a lantern on the small table in the corridor. He dragged a chair from inside his office and placed it beside the table, then sat down and gazed quizzically at his prisoner. Karner lay stretched out on the bunk, staring at the ceiling, with his hands folded across his chest.

Bursofsky reached into a shirt pocket and removed a cigar.

'You still like these?' he asked.

Karner's face brightened. 'Hell, yes, I do.'

The marshal stood up and passed the cigar and a match through the bars to Karner, who sat back down on the cot. He thumb-snapped the lucifer and toasted the edge of the cigar before lighting it. He pulled a large plume of smoke into his mouth and rolled it around before letting it slither out of the right corner of his lips.

'Well, you want to start at the beginning, Steve?' Bursofsky asked. 'You know, I thought you was dead the last few years.'

'I almost was,' Karner said.

'Where you been?'

'Here and there.' Karner's tone wasn't dismissive, but he wanted Bursofsky to know that the discussion wouldn't be on the lawman's terms.

'I can tell you, Steve — lots of folks are going to be real pleased to know you're alive and well.'

'I appreciate that, Marshal.'

Bursofsky rubbed his palms on his pant legs, trying to find a way to penetrate the wall that Karner had erected between them. He fingered another cigar from his pocket and lighted it, watching Karner through the smoke.

The marshal was more than ten years older than Karner, but for some reason he had always looked at the younger man as a peer. Steve Karner was the sort of man who inspired respect like that. Like his uncle, Karner wasn't the talkative sort. He was a man who lived out his principles rather than preaching about them. His values were hard work, loyalty, and a willingness to stand up for what he thought was right, regardless of what others thought. Ash Karner was the same sort of man, and Bursofsky figured Karner's late father had been, too.

The disappearance of Steve Karner had been one of the more perplexing events of Bursofsky's tenure as town marshal of Stayton. Karner's horse had been found in the woods near the river, but there had been no sign of him anywhere. By common consent, he had fallen in and drowned somehow. Most people in town seemed to accept that explanation. However, Ethan Bursofsky never had. It just didn't make sense. How would Karner have fallen in? And if he had fallen in, why had he drowned? He was a very strong swimmer, as everyone familiar with him knew. Something about the whole thing just didn't sit right with the marshal, although he had never been able to find any evidence to confirm his suspicions. Life went on, years passed, and yet Karner's disappearance continued to nag at him.

And now here Steve Karner was, right here in Stayton, sitting in the jail cell, smoking a cigar. He was here because Bursofsky had caught him in the act of trying to kill Phil Taylor. The lawman couldn't help but assume that Karner was responsible for the recent murder spree in town, too.

'What made you leave town to begin with?' asked Bursofsky. It was the best he could come up with at the moment.

'Let's just say it wasn't exactly by choice.'

'How so?'

Karner picked a stray fleck of tobacco off the tip of his tongue. 'I was sent packing against my will.'

'How long you been back? Nobody's seen you around, at least that I know of.'

'Got back a few days ago.'

'You been out to see Ash?'

'Yep.'

'I'll bet he was real happy to see you.'

'He was. I was real happy to see him, too.'

The conversation trailed off momentarily, and Bursofsky felt his patience wearing thin. He didn't want to get angry at Karner, because he knew that wouldn't do him any good as far as getting more information went. Finally he shrugged and rose to his feet.

'It's getting late. I'm going to go to bed. Maybe we can talk more in the morning.'

'That sounds fine, Marshal. I'll see you then.'

Bursofsky dimmed the lantern and went into the front office, closing the cell block door behind him. He had a cot set up near his desk and would be passing the night there.

Karner listened to the thud of the closing door, and then heard Bursofsky lock it behind him. He leaned back on the bunk and puffed again on his cigar. Ten minutes later, he was asleep.

★ ★ ★

The next morning, Marshal Bursofsky sent the boy from the livery out to Ash Karner's spread to let the old man know his nephew was in custody at the Stayton jail. When Ash rode into town that morning, there were dozens of people on the plank sidewalks of Main Street. He could feel their eyes on him as he rode past.

Word travels awful fast around here, he thought.

He alighted in front of the marshal's office and tossed his reins around the hitching post. The door opened and Ethan Bursofsky greeted him.

'Good morning, Ash,' he said. His face was drawn. 'Come on in.'

'Thank you, Marshal,' Ash said. He followed Bursofsky in and waited while the lawman unlocked the door to the cell block.

'I'll let you two talk a spell,' Bursofsky said. He went back into the office and closed the door behind him.

Ash sat down in the chair in front of the barred cell door. 'I heard talk you climbed out of the river and attacked Phil Taylor,' he said.

Karner nodded. 'I was watching his house from across the river. I couldn't approach it from the street without someone seeing me. Old Phil just about filled his drawers when he saw me coming at him.' He laughed, and there was a trace of amusement in Ash's face as he listened to the story. 'I'd have made him talk, too, if his missus hadn't come out to check on him.'

'Were you going to kill him?' asked Ash.

Karner shook his head. 'I know he

knows something. I thought he might like to share it with me. Anyway, we'll have our little chat at a later date. You can bet on that.'

'I wish I could be so optimistic, boy. I think they're going to try to hang you.'

'They can't prove anything, except what Bursofsky saw in Taylor's yard.'

'Word has it Phil Taylor's pa has already spoken to the governor about you trying to kill his boy. They got a lot of connections.' He sighed. 'I guess that could just be a rumor, though.'

Karner's face betrayed no concern over his uncle's words. 'They don't want me telling the real story about what happened that night,' he said evenly. 'I don't know if old Taylor knows that Pete paid those boys to try to kill me. I doubt it.'

'You could tell the marshal what happened,' Ash suggested.

'I'm not going to tell anyone anything until I've killed Pete Taylor.'

Ash couldn't hide his exasperation. 'Now how in hell are you going to kill

Pete Taylor?' He glanced toward the cell block door and lowered his voice. 'He's five hundred miles from here and you're sitting in a jail cell, in case you hadn't noticed.'

'There's more than one way out of here, Ash,' Karner said coolly.

'There is?'

'Yes, there is.' Karner leaned forward on the cot, resting his elbows on his knees. He lowered his voice now, too. 'Here's what we're going to do — '

The key sounded in the cell block door and Karner stopped talking. The hinges creaked and the marshal came into the corridor and stopped near Ash, who stood up.

'They just brought your breakfast over from the café,' Bursofsky said to his prisoner. He looked at Ash. 'I'm afraid visiting time's over, Ash.'

'Not a problem,' the old man said.

'You can come back tomorrow and see him if you'd like.'

'I'll do that.' Ash waved at his nephew. 'You be good,' he said.

Karner grinned. 'I'll try my best.'

Ash turned and walked into the front room. A tray of food sat on the marshal's desk. He opened the door to the street and found himself surrounded by curious locals as he stepped out onto the sidewalk.

'Ash, I hear Steve's alive,' said Cole Shelton, the owner of the hardware store.

Ash scanned the expectant faces, not sure what to say. 'Yeah,' he mumbled. 'He's alive.'

'What's he doing in the jail?' Shelton asked. He appeared to be the spokesman for the six people who stood in a half-circle around Ash Karner.

'Well . . . ' Ash said hesitantly, his face flushed. 'You'll have to ask the marshal. I'm not sure I can talk about it.'

'Rumor has it he's the one who's been killing the boys from the mill.'

'Don't you have some hammers to sell, Cole?' Ash asked, visibly irritated. 'By God, you sound like an old clucking hen.'

A few of the spectators chuckled, embarrassing Shelton.

'Damn, Ash — I was just asking,' he said.

'Maybe try minding your own damn business,' Ash replied. He pushed past Shelton, and the others made room for him. They stood watching him in silence as he mounted and heeled his horse down the street.

As he passed the café, he saw Paul Lockhart standing under the awning. He was dressed in expensive clothes, smoking a cigarette. Ash stared at him for a moment but didn't offer any sort of greeting. Had it been Tom Lockhart, he would have been courteous, but Paul was another breed, and Ash had never liked him. He wondered why the man was standing there staring at him like that, and the thought only further inflamed his annoyance.

Paul Lockhart had never tried to disguise his contempt for most of the human race. He believed that his station in life had been earned rather than bestowed upon him through chance. He was close only to his family, and he interacted with others only from a position of power. His family was by far the wealthiest in town, and his father had powerful allies throughout the state government. Indeed, the elder Lockhart was largely responsible for the election of the last governor — only one example of the influence the family wielded. For common laborers such as Ash Karner, Paul had nothing but disdain and indifference. He expected to be called 'sir', and he was quickly angered if he didn't receive what he considered to be a proper level of deference. This extended even to the family's prominent neighbors on Water Street, most of whom avoided his company whenever they could. Ash figured that Paul Lockhart was quite likely the single most widely disliked man in Stayton, with no close competitors.

'Goddamn rich punks,' he muttered. He thought of Pete Taylor, who appeared to have been the catalyst for the entire mess in which Steve had become embroiled. He wished Pete were still in town, so that his nephew could have settled things once and for all. But now Steve was in jail, and all the powers in town appeared to be aligning against him.

★ ★ ★

The sky was overcast, and Phil Taylor thought its gloominess matched his mood.

He was standing in his father's ornate study, staring out of the window. The trees on the nearby mountains were covered in thick mist. His neck was still sore from where Steve Karner had squeezed it the night before.

The door opened and his father walked in. Arch Taylor wasn't a large man, but his very presence was formidable. He was bald and turning fat, with snow-white hair encircling his shiny dome-like head, and a huge handlebar mustache. His face brightened when he saw his younger son. His relationship with Phil had always been far better than his relationship with Pete. Phil may have lacked his father's rugged self-confidence, but he had always been a respectful boy, responsible and serious about the things that mattered. The same could not be said for Pete.

Arch walked over and gently patted his son's shoulder. 'Glad to see you, son,' he said. 'What the hell happened?'

Phil Taylor recounted the events of the previous night to his father, whose face showed a combination of confusion and stark anger.

'Steve Karner is alive?' he asked. His son nodded. 'And he tried to kill you?'

'That's what it seemed like to me,' Phil said. 'And I think he's the one who killed those men who work for Lock-hart.'

'But why?'

Phil's jaw clenched. This was the moment of truth. But some impulse precluded him from telling the whole story, or at least as much of the story as Pete had shared with him. He didn't want to associate himself with the entire sordid, bloody affair, particularly in his father's mind.

'Pa, it's about Pete.'

Arch Taylor's thick white brows moved closer together. 'Pete?'

'Yes,' said Phil. 'Pete.'

'What do you mean?'

'All I know is what Karner told me,' Phil lied. 'He said Pete had crossed him and that I needed to pay for what he'd done.'

'What's he talking about? What did Pete do?'

Color showed in Arch Taylor's face. Phil knew his father was already thinking the worst about Pete. Serves Pete right, he thought. He brought all this on me. Let him take all of Pa's wrath.

'I don't know what he meant, Pa,' said Phil. 'You'd have to ask Pete.'

Arch Taylor lowered himself into a plush leather chair. His hands gripped the arms of the chair so tightly that his knuckles turned white. He raised his head and gazed at his younger, and favorite, son.

'That's exactly what I'm going to do,' he said steadily, his face determined.

'You're going to ask Pete?'

'Yes, indeed. I'm going to send him a telegram and demand that he come home. He's got a few things he needs to explain to me.'

Phil Taylor tried to suppress a grin, and succeeded. 'What if he won't come?'

'Oh, he'll come,' said Arch. 'You can bet on that, son.'

Phil knew his father was right. There was no way Pete Taylor could refuse a command from the patriarch.

8

Steve Karner had several more visitors after his uncle left.

A few of his old friends from the mill stopped by. They were careful to avoid asking about the murders or the disappearance of Jack Buckley. He was glad to see them, although he realized the person he was now was far removed from the man they had last seen several years ago. Karner now divided his life into two distinct phases — before the night of the attack, and after. He still liked the young men who stood rather awkwardly outside his cell, trying to make small talk. But he didn't feel he had much in common with them anymore. He had the impression they could feel the distance between them, too. They left after fifteen minutes.

A flood of complex emotions filled Karner when Patsy McCurtin's mother and father came to see him that afternoon. The McCurtins owned a small farm about five miles outside town. Patsy had been their only daughter, and Karner was now painfully aware that she had died while searching for him.

Mack McCurtin wasn't an old man, but the death of his daughter and the passing of the years seemed to have aged him considerably. His clothes hung loosely from his body, and his chest was sunken. He was clean shaven and his still-thick hair was neatly combed. Nancy McCurtin, too, seemed much older than her actual years, her white hair pulled back in a pony tail and soft folds of flesh sagging under her eyes. Their faces brightened when they saw Steve Karner, who leapt to his feet and reached through the bars of his cell to grasp their hands.

'Very good to see you both,' he said. His eyes pooled with tears, and then theirs did, too. 'It's been a long time.'

'We heard you were back this morning,' said Mack. 'We had to come and see you. Wish it wasn't under these circumstances, of course, but we've never forgotten how much you meant to our girl, and how much she meant to you, too.'

Patsy's mother squeezed Karner's hand with a strength that belied her haggard appearance. 'You look good, Steven,' she said. 'Tired, but good.'

Karner smiled. 'Thanks, ma'am. I wish our meeting again wasn't like this, but I can't help that now.'

'What happened?' Mack asked.

Karner was vague in his explanation, but he did tell them that he hadn't left Stayton of his own accord. He told them that he had decided to stay away when he learned of Patsy's death.

'I visited her grave the other night,' he said. 'I still can't hardly believe she's gone.'

Mack McCurtin nodded. 'Neither can we,' he said. 'We go out there and visit her every Sunday after church.'

'You know, she sure did think the world of you, Steve Karner,' said Nancy.

113

'You were always real good to her. We'd have been proud to have you as a son-in-law.'

'There's nothing I would have wanted more,' Karner said, his face suddenly ashen. 'I'd have taken good care of Patsy. She deserved it.'

'That she did,' said Mack.

'That's part of why I've come back to Stayton.'

Mack McCurtin arched an eyebrow. 'What do you mean, son?'

'I've come back to take care of a few things. I can't really say more than that. I wish I could, but I can't.'

'They say you might have been involved in those . . . killings,' Nancy said.

Karner looked toward the floor of his cell. 'Don't believe everything you hear,' he said simply.

'We don't,' said Mack firmly. 'Believe you me — we don't.'

'Good.'

The conversation lulled. The McCurtins took their leave, promising to come and visit again.

When they had left, Karner tried to sleep, but his racing mind and the sounds of activity out on Main Street kept him awake. Ethan Bursofsky brought him his lunch but didn't try to get any more information from him. Karner had the impression that Bursofsky was biding his time before he tried to get the prisoner to talk.

He was just finishing his meal when he heard the key rattle in the cell block door. The marshal opened it and made way for yet another visitor. Tom Lockhart walked in and Karner rose. He greeted Lockhart warmly.

'Hell, Tom — didn't expect to see you here. How've you been?'

Bursofsky closed the door and Lockhart shook Karner's hand.

'I've been well, Steve. Real well.' He sat down on the chair outside the cell. 'I can't believe I'm seeing you here, in the flesh. To be honest, almost everybody thought you'd died.'

'I nearly did,' Karner said.

'What do you mean?' Lockhart asked.

Karner paused. He had known Tom Lockhart his entire life, and, like almost everyone in Stayton, he had always liked and respected him. Lockhart had been a good friend during their childhood, seemingly oblivious to the massive social disparity between the orphaned boy and himself. He had also been a friend to Patsy McCurtin, who looked upon Lockhart almost as a brother. Karner didn't doubt that Lockhart had been devastated by Patsy's death. He was almost tempted to give him some of the details about the night he had nearly died, but something caused him to hold back. He hadn't told anyone but Ash, and he decided to keep it that way, at least for the time being.

'It's a long story, Tom,' Karner said. 'Maybe someday I'll be able to tell you everything. I don't plan on staying in this cell forever.'

'I hope not!' Lockhart said, trying to keep the conversation as light as possible under the circumstances. 'I take it the marshal is treating you well.'

'Yes, he is. He's a good man. Just doing his job and such.'

'I understand. I think it's hard for him, what with his being a friend to your uncle for so long.'

'Ash don't hold it against him.'

'What exactly are they holding you for?'

'According to the marshal, it's for attacking Phil Taylor. Sounds like they might charge me with attempted murder.'

'Were you . . . trying to kill him?'

'If I had been,' Karner said, 'he'd be dead right now.' There was no arrogance in his statement.

Lockhart looked relieved. 'So you weren't trying to kill him.'

'Let's just say I wanted the two of us to have a talk. He wasn't too keen on it, and his missus got scared. Bursofsky was riding by and heard her scream, and when he came to see what the ruckus was about, Phil was trying to pull his gun on me. And so here we are.'

Lockhart had a concerned expression on his face as he said, 'I'm sure you've heard about what happened to Patsy.'

'Yes, I did. Her ma and pa came to see me.'

'Patsy was a real special girl,' said Lockhart. 'She always was. If I remember right, you two were going to get married.'

'That was the plan.'

'Any man would have been proud to have her for a wife.'

'I think so, too.'

There was a moment of awkwardness. Lockhart changed the subject. 'So what's going to happen next? Is the marshal going to charge you?'

'They're waiting on a lawyer to come over from the district attorney's office in Salem. That's what he told me this morning. I'll guess we'll wait and see.'

'If there's anything I can do to help, just let me know,' Lockhart said. 'You know I've always liked you and your uncle — '

The door to the front office opened

118

and both men turned to see Paul Lockhart step into the corridor. He walked up to the cell door and smiled at Karner. There was no trace of friendliness in his disdainful eyes.

It had been years since Karner had laid eyes on Paul. He noticed that the man had changed much more in the intervening period than had his twin brother. His hair was thinning at the temples and streaks of premature grey showed in it. There were lines in his face that his brother lacked. But still there was the same arrogance in his expression. Karner thought that Paul Lockhart, unlike Tom, had always had a chip on his shoulder — a strange thing for a boy who had never had to work for anything in his life, and whose involvement in the running of the family business had been peripheral at best and, more often, non-existent. There had always been a contemptuous anger in the man, even when he was a child. He had been a bully — not unlike Pete Taylor. Karner reckoned it was all still there, and wondered why Tom had turned out to be such a different person from Paul.

'Howdy, Paul,' Karner said.

'Karner,' Paul retorted. His appraising eyes looked Karner over, and it seemed he was unimpressed by what he saw. 'Welcome home.'

Karner smirked, staring back at Paul but saying nothing. His greeting was all the words he would waste on the man.

Tom Lockhart could feel the tension. 'We were just finishing our little visit here, Paul,' he said. 'You ready to head on home?'

Paul stared for another moment at Karner, then pivoted and walked down the corridor to the office. Tom looked at Karner apologetically.

'You know how Paul is, Steve,' he said. He shrugged. 'I best be heading out. Maybe I'll come back and see you in a day or two, if you'd like that.'

'I would, Tom,' Karner said. 'Thanks for stopping by.'

They shook hands again and Tom

Lockhart left. Bursofsky closed the connecting door, leaving Karner alone with his thoughts.

★ ★ ★

Marshal Ethan Bursofsky came into the cell block at dusk, carrying Karner's dinner with him. He unlocked the barred door and handed the covered plate over to the prisoner. He wasn't concerned that Karner would try to escape. Karner took the plate gratefully.

'Thanks, Marshal,' he said.

Bursofsky removed a fork from his pocket and handed it through the bars after he closed and locked the cell again.

'One thing you won't be able to say is that we didn't feed you well here in the Stayton jail,' said the marshal. 'You know, old Nelly at the café has always liked you. I think she's making these meals extra tasty.'

Karner laughed and began to eat with a healthy appetite. Bursofsky pulled the chair closer, its legs making scraping noises on the plank floor. He sat down and exhaled wearily.

'You might be interested to know that I got a telegram from the district attorney's office in Salem,' he said. 'Looks like it's going to be four or five days before they're able to send out the prosecutor.'

'I heard the Taylors are going to try to nail me to the wall.'

'Who told you that?'

'Ash.' Karner swallowed a large bite of mashed potatoes. 'He said that was the word going around town.'

'I haven't heard from any of the Taylors,' Bursofsky said. 'Which is kind of surprising, to be honest. We've got a lot of gossips here in Stayton.'

Karner had his own thoughts about the Taylor family's reticence, but chose to keep them to himself. 'What are you planning on charging me with, Marshal?' he asked.

'That depends. You did physically attack Phil Taylor. Two witnesses saw it happening, myself included. But if he's not going to press charges, then I don't know that you'll end up being charged with anything.'

'Suits me fine.'

Bursofsky examined a cuticle on his thumb, considering the words he was about to say. 'I have to ask you, Steve — did you have anything to do with the deaths of Snow, Thompson, or Ballard?'

Karner wiped up some gravy with a chunk of bread and chewed it carefully before he responded. 'What do you think, Marshal? Do you think I killed those fellers?'

'Don't know. But I'm going to tell you the truth — I think it's very possible you did, maybe even likely.'

Karner nodded pensively. 'I can't say I blame you for thinking that.'

'It seems more than coincidental that you would return after years of people thinking you were dead, and then these fellers are each murdered, one after the other.'

'True.'

'And Jack Buckley. Were you two friends?'

'Not quite.'

'Can't blame you there,' Bursofsky said sardonically. 'He ain't the most likeable feller in town.'

Karner raised an eyebrow, letting that speak for itself. 'So it's mostly up to the Taylors, whether I get charged with anything?'

Bursofsky nodded. 'Yeah. We'll have to see what Phil wants to do. My hands are tied, you understand. I saw what I saw and I'll have to testify to that in court if the prosecutor moves forward.' He rose, moving the chair back toward the wall across the corridor from the cell. 'Come to think of it, you aren't the only person who's reappeared all of a sudden.'

'What do you mean?'

'I heard Pete Taylor's in town.'

Karner stepped forward and clutched the bars of his cell, his face coloring. 'What did you say?'

'Pete Taylor,' said Bursofsky, slightly

taken aback by Karner's sudden intensity. He frowned. 'Everything alright, Steve?'

Karner seemed to looking through him rather than at him.

'Yes, sir,' he said softly. 'Everything's just fine.'

9

Pete Taylor alighted from the railway carriage, pulling his hat brim down over his face. His eyes were wary as they moved over the station platform. He hadn't been home in years, and although he was in Salem now rather than Stayton, he felt like someone might recognize him here.

Why the hell should I care, he thought defiantly. I'm a Taylor. Nobody can touch me, and they better watch their mouths if they want to say something smart to me.

He often bolstered his confidence like this. Despite his outward bravado, he had never felt sure of himself or his place in the world. Much of his insecurity stemmed from his father. Taylor knew that he and his father had never had a good relationship, and as his problems with gambling and women intensified in early adulthood, his father's disapproval had become more and more undisguised. This had only served to make the young man's behavior less respectable, as if the only way he could assert his individuality was to offend his father.

The telegram his father had sent him had startled him as few things had in his life. Steve Karner was alive, and he had tried to kill Phil. It was almost incomprehensible that Karner could have survived that attack. When he had contacted Phil for more information, he had learned about the deaths of Clarence Snow, Gil Thompson, Dave Villiers and Norm Ballard, as well as the disappearance of Jack Buckley. Pete Taylor didn't have a penetrating mind, but he was smart enough to know that it must have been Steve Karner who killed those men, and he must also have been responsible for whatever happened to Buckley. And the only reason Karner could have had for attacking Phil was that he knew of Pete's involvement in the attempt on his life.

Taylor had gone over these things time and time again in the two days that had passed since his father's telegram had reached him. He had scarcely slept since. The nervous tension within him was almost unbearable, but his native arrogance helped him maintain control of his anxieties — for now. His main fear was the possibility that Karner had told someone else that Pete Taylor was behind that ambush in the woods, all those years ago.

But there was more to it than that. If he was going to go down for the crime, then he would make sure he wasn't the only one to take the blame. Because it hadn't been his idea to begin with. He had been paid to do it, and there was no way he could decline the offer he had received, or at least that was how it had seemed at the time. He had been vulnerable, and when the man approached him, promising him $5,000 to set up Karner's murder, he had been willing to do anything to avoid letting his father know about his new gambling debts, and about the men who had threatened his life if he didn't settle with them. The potential for disgrace would have turned his father against him forever.

A freezing November wind blew across the platform, and Taylor shivered. He pushed the troubling thoughts from his mind. He had purposely chosen to come in on a late-night train so that no one would know he was coming back home — at least not right away. He hefted his valise and walked into the station, again looking for any familiar faces. He saw none and continued out onto the street. Despite the street lamps, it was very dark out. He decided he would find a hotel for the night, and then make his way to Stayton tomorrow in his own good time. The old man had been ordering him around his whole life. Let him sweat a little.

He found an expensive hotel near the station and checked in. The next morning, he rented a horse and rode east toward Stayton.

*　　*　　*

There was a drizzling rain coming down when Pete Taylor rode up the road to his father's house, in the forested hills outside Stayton. He pulled leather near the porch and looked around.

Nothing had changed in the years since he had left. The giant house, built of logs and river rock, was just as imposing and neatly maintained as it had always been. The grounds were tidy, and he could hear sounds of activity and men's voices coming from the stables. This was the Taylor place — the home of one of the most prominent and wealthy families in this part of the state of Oregon. Pete Taylor had been born and raised here. But it had never really felt like home to him.

He dismounted with a strange feeling of foreboding stirring within him. He was about to face his father, and that had always caused him discomfort. Now he didn't want to imagine the sorts of questions his father was going to ask him. The old man had summoned him home, and it was because of the return of Steve Karner. What could he tell his father about what had happened all those years ago, and why he had been a part of it? He felt a cold tingle in the back of his neck.

He mounted the steps and gripped the wrought iron door handle. When he opened the door, he saw that the foyer was empty. He closed the door behind him and looked up the staircase to the landing on the second floor. Standing there with his hands on the banister was his younger brother, Phil. His expression was notably cold.

Pete smiled, because he didn't know what else to do. 'Howdy there, Phil!' he said.

'Pete,' his brother replied. There wasn't a trace of warmth in his voice.

Pete took a deep breath and looked toward the closed doors of his father's study. How many times he stood in that room, wincing under yet another of his father's tongue lashings? He raised his eyes again to Phil.

'Pa around?' he asked.

Phil shook his head. 'He's up at the logging camp. He won't be back until this evening.'

There was a look of unalloyed relief on Pete's face. 'What about Ma?' he asked.

'She's sleeping,' said Phil. 'You know, her health ain't the best.'

'Hell, I know that,' Pete retorted indignantly.

Phil stared down at his brother for a few more seconds, then moved to the steps and descended to the ground floor. Despite the chilly reception he had given his brother, Phil extended his hand and shook Pete's. He jerked his head toward their father's study.

'Let's go have a drink and talk, Pete,' he said.

Pete Taylor agreed eagerly and followed his brother into the room. There were several overstuffed leather chairs near the windows that overlooked the forests surrounding the property on all sides. The drizzling rain continued to fall, making soft pattering sounds against the window panes. Phil walked over to the bar and splashed brandy in a pair of tumblers, one of which he handed to Pete. He took the other and stood near the windows.

'This is a hell of a mess, Pete,' he said somberly. 'A hell of a mess.'

'I know it,' Pete said, gazing down in the swirling liquid in his glass. 'Who the hell knew Karner would live?'

'Well, he did. There's no getting around it.'

'What did you tell Pa?'

'Nothing,' Phil said. 'All I told him was that Karner asked me about you when he attacked me.'

'Why the hell did you tell him that?!'

Phil looked at his brother with disgust. 'Because of you, Pete, that son of a bitch tried to kill me in my back yard. Do you realize that?'

'Yes, I do.'

'It ain't my damn job to make excuses to Pa for you. What did you expect me to tell him? He wanted to know why Karner attacked me.'

'Tell him you don't know!'

'He wouldn't have bought that. And we don't know what Karner has told the marshal. Have you thought about that?'

'Every day I've thought about that!'

'Have you thought about the fact that I almost got killed because of your stupid ass?'

Pete started to say something but changed his mind. He put the tumbler to his lips and poured half the brandy into his mouth. His eyes watered from its potency.

'I'm sorry about that, Phil. Honest. I never thought that would happen.'

Phil sipped at his drink. 'This could destroy our family. It goes far beyond you now. You've never been responsible or given a damn about whether others were hurt by the asinine decisions you've made.'

'That's not true — '

'Shut up, Pete!'

Pete Taylor jumped to his feet. 'You ain't going to talk to me like that, Phil. I'm your older brother. Don't forget that.'

Phil met his brother's gaze. 'I'll talk to you any way I please.' His eyes didn't waver, and after a moment Pete sat back down.

'How did you get involved in all this, Pete? You've never really told me the whole story.'

Pete polished off the liquor and held out the glass for a refill. Phil got it for him and then stood by, waiting to hear what his brother had to say. Pete swallowed some more of it before he began to speak.

'I got into some serious trouble,' he said. 'I got into a poker game in Portland with Cobb McGillicutty. The game was going my way, and I put every penny I had into it.'

'And then you lost.'

Pete paused. 'Yes,' he said presently. 'I know McGillicutty cheated, the son of a bitch!'

Phil Taylor was unimpressed. 'You should

have known he'd cheat before you started playing high stakes with him.'

'I know that now, Phil.'

'Were you drunk?'

Another pause. 'Yeah, I was drunk.'

'Of course.' Phil sighed. 'So you lost all that money — and what happened then?'

'I came back home and asked Pa to help me. He got so angry he cut me off. Told me he'd never give me another penny as long as I lived. I always felt like he hated me somehow, but after that meeting, I *knew* it. His own son — and he's never given a good goddamn about me.'

'Can you blame him, Pete? I mean, really?'

Pete Taylor scrubbed a hand across his jaw. 'I told him they were going to kill me if I didn't get that money. He told me to go to hell.' He looked toward his brother. 'I damn near asked Ma for it. She'd have given it to me.'

Phil's eyes widened. 'That would have been the dumbest thing you ever did in your life.'

'I know it. That's why I didn't go through with it. I just thought about it.'

'A wise choice, for once.'

'You want to hear this story or make more wise-ass remarks?'

'I'm sorry,' Phil said. 'Go on.'

'After Pa turned me down, I went into Stayton and got tanked at the saloon. I guess I was running my mouth a little too much, got a little too free with the information I was imparting. I left the saloon and was going through the alley to the livery when someone stopped me and told me they could help me find a way out of my problems. But they wanted something in exchange.'

'What did . . . they want?'

'They wanted Steve Karner dead. And they didn't want anyone to know who was behind it. I would get five thousand dollars if I set it up, free and clear. All I had to do was make sure Karner was dead and that I never *ever* mentioned the name of the person who paid me for it.'

'And you agreed.'

'Ain't that obvious by now? Hell yes, I agreed. I'd be dead right now if I hadn't. I talked to Norm Ballard, Gil Thompson, and Dave Villiers. I guess Gil ran his mouth, because next thing I know Jack Buckley and Clarence Snow volunteered to help, the mean-spirited bastards.'

'Did Gil tell anyone else?'

'No, not that I know of. Villiers wasn't sure he wanted to take part, but I told him he'd lose his job if he didn't. He was about ready to get fired anyway; he was always missing work and drunk off his ass. Ballard and Thompson were ready to do it from the second I asked them. They were always short of money.'

'How did you pick those boys to do the killing?'

'They were . . . suggested to me.'

'Who by?'

'By the feller who hired me to set the whole damn thing up, that's who.'

Phil Taylor refilled his tumbler and

then walked to a chair near his brother's. He sat down, his face drawn.

'Who was it, Pete?' he asked. 'You didn't tell me before, but I have to know.'

'Why? You don't need to know nothing. You ain't helped me none!'

'Goddamn it — who was it? You don't tell me and I'll take this up with Pa, by God. You hear?'

Pete Taylor slumped in his chair, his shoulders sagging. For the first time his brother could remember, he looked defeated — utterly defeated. All his years of careless debauchery had caught up with him, and there was no way out.

Pete's rheumy eyes flicked over to Phil. A small grin quirked the corners of his lips.

'You really don't know who it was?' he asked. He chuckled quietly. 'I thought you'd have figured it out by now, little brother.'

'Well, you thought wrong, Pete. Who the hell wanted Karner dead?'

Pete gazed out at the trees on the

hillside beyond the windows. When he spoke, his voice was subdued yet malevolent.

'Lockhart.'

10

Ash Karner was waiting on the stoop in front of the jail the next morning when Bursofsky opened the door to fetch breakfast for his prisoner.

'Well, you're here early, Ash,' Bursofsky said amiably.

'I got a few things I need to talk to Steve about,' explained Ash. He seemed oddly agitated, in a way Bursofsky had never seen before.

The marshal gestured for Ash to follow him inside, then opened the door into the cell block.

'I'm going to get his breakfast,' he said. 'I trust you're not going to help him escape or anything like that.' He smiled as he said it, but the remark only seemed to make Ash more jumpy.

'No, no — nothing like that. Just wanted to talk about . . . family business and such. You understand.'

'Yes, yes,' Bursofsky said, his eyes searching Ash's grizzled face. 'Family business.' He turned back toward the front door. 'I'll be back in a few minutes.'

'Much obliged, Marshal,' Ash said. He watched Bursofsky exit out onto the sidewalk, then hurried in to talk to his nephew. He found him sitting on the edge of the bunk in his cell. 'You're never going to believe who's in town.'

Karner grinned crookedly. 'Pete Taylor.'

'How'd you know?' Ash seemed slightly annoyed.

'Bursofsky told me last night. How'd you find out?'

'Wes Tancred saw him riding up the hill to his pa's place yesterday. Evidently he skirted town. I'll bet he doesn't want word getting around. Well, it's too late for that.'

'There's only one reason his sorry ass would come back,' Karner asserted. 'And that's because he heard I'm back, and he's scared. He knows what happened to the lowdown bushwhackers he hired to kill me.'

'Yep, that's what I figured, too.'

Karner stretched, trying to relieve some of the tension swirling within him. 'I got to get out of here, Ash,' he said. 'I've got to move now, while Pete's still in town, and while he still thinks I'm in jail.'

'Fair enough. But how?'

Karner looked up at the ceiling of his cell. 'You remember when I helped work on this place?'

'Yeah, I do.'

Karner gestured toward a dark circular outline on the floor near the corner of the cell. 'This used to be the front office, before the town paid to expand the jail.' He walked over to the dark area. 'There used to be a wood stove here, with a chimney leading up through the roof.'

Ash raised his eyes to the ceiling directly above the spot on the floor. 'All right, what's your plan, boy?'

'The roof in this corner is nothing but plywood. When they took the stove and chimney out, they just covered it with a flat board.' He lowered his gaze to his uncle. 'You could get up there tonight and bust through it. Lower me a rope and I'll be out of here in five minutes. You follow me?'

Ash swallowed, considering the plan. 'I follow you. But what about the marshal? Ain't he been sleeping in the front room?'

'Yeah, but he sleeps like a log. The other night someone tried to fetch him and they almost had to break down the front door before he woke up. I don't think he'll know a thing till the morning.'

'I hope you're right.'

'Trust me. He won't be a problem.'

Ash hitched his thumbs into the pockets of his pants. 'When do you want to do this?' he asked.

'Tomorrow at midnight will work.'

'All right, then. Midnight tomorrow it is.'

They heard Bursofsky's boots thudding on the steps. The conversation was over. The marshal entered with Karner's breakfast, and Ash took his leave, his pulse pounding in his ears.

A man from the logging camp arrived at the Taylor house to tell Phil and Pete that their father wouldn't be coming home that night. There was pressing business he had to attend to. Pete was grateful for the reprieve. He spent much of the afternoon visiting his invalid mother, and then he joined Phil for dinner in the dining room. They said little, and then after eating, Phil left to return home to his wife in Stayton. He promised to come back the next morning.

Pete drank several more glasses of his father's expensive liquor and fell asleep on the sofa in the study. The sunlight streaming through the windows didn't awaken him, but an insistent nudging against his leg did.

'Pete, wake up. Wake up, goddamn it!'

Pete slowly opened his eyes and saw Phil standing before him.

'Good God, you smell like you fell

into a vat of whiskey,' Phil said disapprovingly. 'I'll have the maid bring in some coffee. We need to talk.'

'About what?'

'You'll see soon enough. Now sit up and try to pull yourself together.'

Phil went out of the room, returning several minutes later with a tray containing a pot of coffee and two cups. He poured for them both, and then handed a cup over to his brother, who was clearly suffering from a severe hangover.

The hot coffee scalded Pete Taylor's tongue. He squinted over the steam rising from his cup and glared at Phil.

'What do you want to talk about? I told you everything yesterday.'

Phil put his cup down on the tray. 'I was up all night, thinking about what we should do,' he said. 'I'm glad Pa didn't come home last night, because he wouldn't approve of this.'

'Approve of what?'

'My plan,' Phil said in a self-satisfied tone that grated on Pete's nerves.

Pete took another sip of the coffee. 'All right, then. Let's hear about your plan,' he said.

'We need to get you out of here. Permanently. You need to go far away, where no one could ever find you. And you can never come back to Stayton again.'

'That's your plan?' Pete asked.

'Yep, that's it.'

'I ain't got the money to go somewhere 'far away' and start all over.'

'I'll take care of that. I'll give you the money. But you have to keep your end of the bargain.'

Pete's eyes were mere slits as he regarded Phil. 'How much money are we talking about?'

Phil shrugged. 'Ten thousand, for starters. That should get you wherever you want to go and allow you to get established in the . . . manner to which you are accustomed.'

'Where you going to get this money?' Pete asked. 'Pa sure as hell ain't going to give it to you.'

'Pete, I have money. Lots of money.'

Pete sneered resentfully. 'Yeah, you've been well taken care of, haven't you, Phil?'

'I work for my money, Pete. Pa wouldn't be able to run the business if I weren't around. Now, are you saying you won't take the money if it comes from me?'

'Nah, I ain't saying that.'

'Good.'

'But why you being so generous? You ain't never lifted a finger for me before.'

'This is a whole lot bigger than just you, Pete. This could bring down our whole family. It could destroy everything Pa has spent the last thirty-five years building. If people knew you took money to set up a murder for someone . . . the disgrace would kill Ma.' Pete's eyes lowered to the floor as Phil spoke. 'This is the only way, Pete. I can send you more money down the line, within reason.'

'Where the hell will I go?' Pete said, and the way he said it made it plain that he was warming to the plan.

'I hear good things about Chicago,' Phil said. 'New Orleans. Hell, you've never been to New York City, have you?'

'No, I haven't.'

'You know, you might have to change your name, too, Pete.'

'That's a bit much, ain't it?'

'I don't think so. They got detective agencies — people could find you if you're not real careful.'

Pete's coffee was cooler now, and he finished it in two gulps. 'But what are we going to do about Steve Karner?' he asked.

'I've thought about that, too,' Phil explained. 'You leave tomorrow. I'll get the money and have it delivered to you at your hotel in a locked box. Then I'll go to the jail and have a talk with Karner, one on one.'

'And say what?'

'That I won't press charges against him if he leaves our family alone. I'll tell him you high-tailed it out of town with a bunch of Pa's money, and that no one

149

has any idea of where you went. I'll even offer him some money to leave us alone. He wanted you, Pete — that's the only reason he came for me. Maybe I'll tell him you headed back up to Seattle or something. He can go up there and look for you, not knowing you're halfway to Kansas City, or wherever. I'm pretty sure he knows I wasn't involved in setting him up.'

'You think he'll go for it?' asked Pete in a pensive tone.

'I can be pretty persuasive,' said Phil. 'And what other choice do we have?'

'None that I can see. But that leaves one other person.'

'Who's that?'

'Lockhart.'

'Hmmm. He's probably sweating bullets right now. The word is all over town that you've come back.'

'It is?'

'Yes, it is. He knows you hold all the cards, Pete. I don't think we'll have to worry about him. He definitely doesn't want you to do any talking. He'll be happy to hear that you skipped out, I'm sure.'

'He's a cold-blooded bastard. He used me so that nothing could ever be traced back to him.'

'Why'd he want Karner dead to begin with?'

'He wanted Patsy,' said Pete. 'Said he'd hated Steve Karner his whole life.'

'You never know about people. Pa always used to say that.'

'I just hope this all works.'

'It will — if you follow the plan. If you go east and change your name, people won't know anything. They'll never find you, as long as you cover your tracks real good.'

'I can do that.'

'You better be sure you can. Like I said, this could destroy us all.' Phil glanced at the clock on the wall above his father's desk. 'You should leave after lunch. You never know when Pa might get back.'

11

Goddamn rain, thought Pete Taylor. Every time I get on a horse it starts raining.

It was late in the evening as Taylor approached Salem in the cold November darkness. He was pondering the mixed emotions he had felt ever since his brother had explained the plan. On the one hand, he had been away from Stayton for years already, so being banished forever didn't make much of a difference to him. On the other hand, it rubbed him the wrong way to have his little brother giving orders to him and making arrangements that Pete would have to follow for the rest of his life.

Pete Taylor ain't no saint, he thought, but Arch Taylor cut a lot of corners and broke more than a few heads over the years while establishing the family empire. Arch had always played to win, and he had never shown the slightest compunction about doing whatever he had to do to get what he wanted. He had always taken care, though, to ensure that his public image was largely untarnished. It had always disgusted Pete, who knew what his father was capable of. And it looked like Phil was going to follow in their father's footsteps, without the slightest hint of any qualms. As always, Phil would do what was good for Phil, and everyone else be damned.

The rain dripped off the brim of his Stetson as he entered town. If there was one element to the plan that he savored it was the thought of never having to lay eyes on his father again. He was relieved that he hadn't had to meet with him. His entire childhood had been spent on the receiving end of Arch Taylor's infuriated tirades. He never wanted to hear another one of the man's smug monologues again. Phil, he could also take it or leave it, despite the fact that his younger brother had found a way for Pete to escape punishment for his involvement in the attempt on Steve Karner's life. The only person he felt a tinge of regret at not seeing again was his mother. She was the one person in his family who had always acted like she loved him.

Tears pooled in his eyes, and he brushed them away angrily. There was no use in becoming emotional, because it was all over and done with now. He would take the money his brother gave him and go far away. He might even take Phil's advice and start using a new name. If the Taylors wanted no part of him, then they could keep their damn name. He didn't need it.

He turned north up the muddy street. The lights of his hotel were visible in the distance, as were those of the train station. All he wanted was a shot of rye and a good night's sleep. Maybe tomorrow he would take a bath before the money arrived.

He drew reins behind the hotel and handed his horse over to the man who operated the small livery there.

'See that he gets oats and lots of water,' Taylor commanded. 'And brush him good, you hear?'

'Yes, sir,' said the man deferentially. 'I'll see to it.'

Taylor walked around to the front of the hotel and went into the lobby. The clerk behind the desk rose.

'How are you, Mr. Taylor?'

'Fine. I'm going to bed now. I think I'll have a hot bath in the morning.'

'Of course, sir. Would you like someone to wake you up at a certain time?'

'Eight'll work fine,' Taylor said. He was always curt with the help; it was just one of the many traits he shared with his father.

He turned and mounted the steps, then walked down the hallway to the door of his room. The lanterns mounted on the wall brackets had been turned down. He noticed this idly as he slipped his key into the lock.

He stepped across the threshold and closed the door. As he locked it, he suddenly became aware of the aroma of cigar smoke. He sniffed a couple of times, his brows knitted together. Who the hell had smoked a cigar in his room?

'Good evening, Mr. Taylor,' said an oily voice from the darkness across the room.

Taylor pivoted, naked fear enveloping him. His hand moved toward the pistol on his hip, but the voice spoke again and he froze in place.

'I wouldn't lay a finger on that pistol if I were you,' it said.

'I won't,' said Taylor hoarsely.

'Good, good. Now be a nice feller and light that lamp on the dresser.'

Taylor fished a match from his shirt pocket and scraped it on the wall. He lighted the lantern.

'Turn up the wick,' the voice intoned.

Taylor obeyed. Now he could see the man — medium-sized, clean-shaven and nondescript, with eyes that seemed to glow expectantly as they regarded Pete Taylor. In the man's right hand was a Remington pistol. The man smiled, and it was the least friendly smile Taylor had ever seen in his life.

'Have a seat,' said the man, gesturing toward the bed. 'We're going to have a little talk.'

Taylor walked to the bed and sat down, careful to keep his hands away from the gun in his holster. He tried to swallow but his mouth was too dry. All the imperiousness had been drained out of him.

'Who sent you?' he asked, almost afraid of the answer.

'Lockhart,' the stranger replied. He noticed the fear in Taylor's face and found it amusing. 'Does that surprise you?'

'No. I guess it doesn't.'

'I didn't think it would.' The man smoothed a wrinkle out of his lapel, seeming perfectly at ease. 'Now, there's one thing Mr. Lockhart would like to know.'

'What's that?' said Taylor, his voice now scarcely more than a whisper.

The flinty eyes stabbed at Taylor.

'Who have you told about his involvement in the little . . . incident from a few years back?'

'Nobody,' Taylor said.

The man's lips spread into a skeptical smirk. 'Come, come, Taylor. You don't expect me to believe that, do you?'

'It's the truth!'

'Why did you come back to Stayton? Why now?'

'Because Karner tried to kill my brother. My father wanted me here.'

'So you're a daddy's boy, are you?' The smirk was still there, taunting and self-assured.

'No, I ain't no daddy's boy. But I wanted to know what was going on, too. Those boys I hired to kill Karner told me there was no way he could be alive.'

'That's the problem with hiring amateurs,' said the man. 'You can't be sure of the quality of their work.'

'Well, I know that now. And I guess Lockhart does, too.'

'Yes, he does. That's why he hired me

this time. Now, again — and this is the last time I'm going to ask. Who else have you told?'

Beads of perspiration were on Taylor's upper lip, and he wiped them away.

'Mister, I'm telling you the truth. I didn't tell a damn soul about Lockhart.'

The man pursed his lips thoughtfully, nodding slowly. 'Fair enough,' he said. There was a tone of finality in the words.

'Did Lockhart send you here to kill me?' Taylor queried, wiping with his sleeve some more sweat from his face.

'Not necessarily.'

'How — how much is he paying you?'

'His family is quite rich, and he can afford to be generous.'

'Whatever it is, I'll double it,' Taylor said urgently. 'Just let me go. I haven't spilled the beans about Lockhart.'

'You'll double it?' There was a softening in the man's face, and Taylor reckoned he had found a chink in his armor.

'You bet.'

The man ran a finger along his jaw-line. He was silent for a moment, and then he nodded. 'That's a lot of money,' he said. 'When could you pay me?'

'Tomorrow afternoon — guaranteed.'

The man pushed himself to a standing position, holding the pistol down at his side. He pulled back the side of his coat and put the gun into a holster there. He looked at Taylor, whose face showed relief.

'The only problem is I got things to do tomorrow afternoon,' said the man. 'Thanks for the offer, though.'

'What?' Taylor sputtered.

He watched as a knife slid out of the man's right sleeve into his palm. Before Taylor could utter another word or cry out, the man took two steps, closing the distance between them, and rammed the knife up under Taylor's chin. As the point of the blade entered his brain, Taylor made a soft grunting noise, his eyes rolling back in his head.

The killer, whose name was Clint

McCall, pulled the knife out and pushed the body backward onto the bed. He wiped the blade on the blankets and replaced it in the thin sheath strapped to his forearm. He straightened his jacket and walked to the door, taking one last look at Pete Taylor's body before leaving.

He had three other men to kill before tomorrow night.

★ ★ ★

McCall had been a professional killer for nearly a decade. His name was on wanted dodgers from Albuquerque to Tacoma, and yet very few persons had any idea of what he looked like, or whether 'Clint McCall' was his real name. In fact, it was — but he had used more than a dozen other pseudonyms in the course of his career.

He wasn't a man who robbed banks, or raped women, or held up stage coaches. He was a killer, and he limited his practice only to high-paying clients with delicate problems for which the only solution was a man of McCall's talents. His record was impeccable; not once had he failed to carry out a murder for which he had been hired, and not once had one of his kills been traced back to the person who had hired him. This made him an extremely valuable commodity.

Among lawmen throughout the West, he had become an almost legendary figure.

Some doubted he even existed. That was exactly the way McCall liked it. It simplified things for him. He had never been careless and he executed his tasks with discretion and total ruthlessness. He had only one rule: no children. He preferred to kill with a gun, but if a knife was necessary to avoid detection, then he would use it without hesitation.

He had learned long ago that he would frequently have to work around the idiosyncrasies of those who hired him. Sometimes they wanted him to let the person know who had sent him before he killed him or her. Sometimes they specifically requested the use of a knife rather than a gun, although McCall refused to torture those he killed. If a customer demanded that he break bones or slash the intended target, then McCall simply declined to work for the person, no matter how great the money. For Clint McCall, killing was a job for which he was very well paid. No more, no less. It wasn't a calling, but rather something he had discovered he had a talent for, and for which there was a sizeable demand. Killing was his business, and business was good.

When he had agreed to take the job from the man calling himself 'Mr. Lockhart,' he had demanded a significantly higher payment than he usually did. He disliked jobs that involved killing more than one person, mostly because they were much more dangerous than single-person jobs. In this case, the cost was also higher because of the urgency with which Lockhart, who had contacted McCall through a mutual acquaintance, wanted the killings to be carried out. Again, this made things much more risky for McCall, and so he had named a price that he thought would probably be rejected — and the mysterious Lockhart had agreed readily to paying it, and even to adding a few thousand extra dollars if the work was carried out to his satisfaction. McCall had never had a customer with this much money to burn, and who was this desperate to hire his services. So he had agreed. The money involved was simply too much to pass up.

The entire thing had been set up through the intermediary. McCall didn't even know what this Lockhart feller's first name was. Just that afternoon he had arrived in Salem, a bank statement guaranteeing Lockhart's payment in his pocket. He had been through the Oregon capitol many times over the years, and he was even familiar with Stayton. The job was proceeding smoothly, now that he had located and eliminated Pete Taylor. Lockhart's written instructions (which

McCall had burned after reading) had asked for the killing of three other men. It didn't state the reasons the men were to be killed, and McCall wasn't particularly curious. Early in his career he had taken an interest in such things, but, almost invariably, he had discovered that people's motives for having others killed were typically mundane or even petty. So he had stopped taking such an interest.

It was the middle of the afternoon when McCall rode into Stayton. He rode up Main Street, refreshing the layout of the town in his mind. He planned to leave the area quickly once he had completed the job. He rode past the telegraph office, the livery, the dry goods store, a few saloons, a church, and four cafés. Near the end of the street were the general store, a hotel, and the marshal's office, with the jail behind it. He had paid close attention to the cross streets, and at the very end of the thoroughfare, just before you ran into the river, was Water Street. McCall grinned slightly, then neck-reined his mount and rode back toward the nearest café. He would eat and spend the rest of the afternoon in town. When nightfall came, he would strike — swiftly and lethally. Then he would be gone, and there would almost surely be no inkling among any of the locals that Clint McCall had ever come to town.

12

Phil Taylor was awake. He had been sleeping soundly, but something had brought him to consciousness. His first thought was of Steve Karner, but he dismissed it as ridiculous. Karner was in jail. In fact, Taylor was planning to go see him the next day, to tell him that Pete had skipped town and to offer a deal if Karner would leave the Taylors alone.

Taylor sighed and looked over at his wife. Amelia was slumbering peacefully, her coppery hair spread out on the pillow around her head. They had gone to bed early. Moonlight streamed through the windows and Taylor thought that she looked as beautiful tonight as she had the day they were married, nearly five years ago. She was the reason he was willing to make such sacrifices to preserve the family's honor and status.

She deserved no less. If he had to pay off Pete and possibly Karner, then so be it. It was worth every penny. Besides, Amelia was a Lockhart. If the Taylors were destroyed, the Lockharts would be, too. Phil Taylor never wanted her to know that her brother had set the entire disastrous fiasco in motion to begin with.

Suddenly a noise downstairs caught his attention, and he sat up in bed, his glance fixed on the half-open bedroom door. Perhaps it was the cat, he thought. His breathing was shallow as he sat there, listening intently. Minutes passed, but there were no further noises. Finally, he relaxed and lay back on his pillow. Soon he was fast asleep.

His dreams were troubled. He imagined the attack on Steve Karner, five men falling upon him, beating him with rocks and sticks and fists. He relived the moment when that dark, almost satanic shape had climbed up out of the river and lunged for him. The past week had been a nightmare, and he had learned many secrets about his family and his community that he would much rather have never learned.

Phil Taylor was still submerged in these unconscious thoughts when Clint McCall slowly pushed the bedroom door open, revealing the two sleeping figures beneath the blankets. McCall stood in the doorway, watching them in silence. He could hear their steady breathing. He had left his boots downstairs, near the bottom of the staircase.

He had already drawn his pistol, and now he took a step forward into the room. He hadn't expected to find the woman in the house, but there was no going back. Lockhart had made no mention of the woman in his instructions; McCall would have to take care of her now, without Lockhart's input. He moved stealthily. In seconds, he was beside the bed, standing over the woman. In one swift motion, he pulled the pillow out from under her head and placed it over her face. He pressed the muzzle of his pistol against the pillow and fired a muffled shot directly into her head.

Phil Taylor sat bolt upright, his eyes bulging. He looked down at the pillow that covered his wife; gun smoke drifted up through the hole where McCall had fired. Then he raised his eyes to Clint McCall, who stared impassively across the bed at him.

'Mr. Lockhart sends his regards,' McCall said.

Taylor's mouth opened as if to scream. McCall pointed his weapon at the gaping hole and fired. Blood and brain matter exploded from the back of Taylor's head, and he tumbled backwards onto the floor beside the bed.

McCall slipped his pistol into its holster and made his way downstairs. He put his boots back on and exited the house through the back door. He stood for a few minutes on the porch until he was satisfied that none of the neighbors had been alerted by the shooting. Then he walked to the big apple tree on the side of the house and untethered his horse. He mounted and rode off into the darkness.

★ ★ ★

At ten o'clock, Marshal Ethan Bursofsky decided he wanted a beer. He sometimes left the marshal's office at night for a few minutes, making sure to lock up while he was gone, in order to take a last look around Main Street before hitting the sack. He liked to check in on the saloon and take a quick stroll down the wide alley that ran behind the businesses on the east side of the street. He didn't do this every night, but he did it probably four or five nights a week.

He put a couple more pieces of firewood in the office stove, then unlocked the door to the cell block and walked down the corridor to check on Steve Karner. The prisoner was stretched out on his bunk, evidently asleep. Bursofsky wasn't worried that Karner would make an escape attempt while the marshal was out, but he wanted to make sure everything was nice and quiet.

He turned and went back into the office, closing and locking the door behind him. He went out onto the sidewalk and locked the front door as well. His eyes scanned Main Street. As usual at this time of night, it was immersed in darkness, with the exception of the three saloons. Even though they were relatively quiet. Stayton wasn't a rowdy town. It was populated mostly by respectable citizens. Only rarely was Bursofsky required to draw his pistol or put someone in the jail, and usually this involved drunken loggers or mill workers who had had a bit too much bourbon and started a fight.

The marshal took a deep breath. He could smell the river in the clean night air. He turned to the right and walked toward the nearest saloon, his boots echoing on the planks of the sidewalk.

When he reached the saloon, he shouldered through the batwings and took a look around. It was populated by the usual clientele — a couple of the local drunks, some boys from the mill, and a logger or two. The atmosphere was subdued, which suited Bursofsky just fine.

He noticed a stranger standing at the bar, nursing a shot glass of whiskey. The man was well dressed and obviously not a laborer. He was clean shaven and his eyes were almost startlingly pale as they returned the marshal's gaze in the mirror behind the bar.

Bursofsky walked toward the man and leaned on the bar about three feet from him. The bartender walked over and stood before the lawman.

'What'll it be, Marshal?' he asked.

'Just a beer, please, Jake,' said Bursofsky. 'Making my last rounds for the night.'

The bartender nodded and filled a glass for Bursofsky. The marshal took it and pulled a large swig, wiping away foam from his lips with the back of his hand. He turned to the stranger and smiled.

'This your first time in Stayton,

pard?' he asked.

Clint McCall turned his eyes to Bursofsky and shook his head. 'Been here before a few times,' he said. 'It's been a few years since I passed through, though.'

'Hmmm,' Bursofsky said. 'What brings you to town?' His tone was deliberately casual.

'On my way to Portland,' said McCall. 'I thought I'd wet my whistle before I rode on.'

Bursofsky had no reason to be suspicious of the man, but there was something about him that was faintly menacing. Perhaps it was his eyes; the marshal wasn't sure. The man wasn't bothering anyone, but for some reason he made Bursofsky wonder what his business was. He thought this over as he took another gulp of beer. He decided he was probably wrong to suspect the man. His imagination had gotten a little more elaborate after the killings and the subsequent arrest of Steve Karner. He finished his beer and set the glass down on the counter.

'Thanks, Jake,' he said to the bartender. He turned to the stranger. 'You have yourself a good trip up to Portland, mister.'

'Thank you kindly, Marshal,' said the man. 'I'll do that.'

Bursofsky walked to the batwings and pushed through them to the sidewalk. He walked up the street, moving north. He took his time, checking the locks on the doors of the closed shops as he went. Further down the street were two other saloons, but he rarely walked that far. They were quiet tonight, as usual.

He had walked about a third of the way up Main Street when he turned right into a narrow walkway between the blacksmith's shed and the hardware store. He walked through to the alley that paralleled Main Street and turned right, heading back in the direction of the combined marshal's office and jail. Moonlight spilled through the branches of the leafless trees to his left as he made his leisurely way back. He checked the back doors of the various establishments, making sure they were locked, too.

He had nearly reached the back of the saloon when he noticed something moving in the shadows. He paused and tilted his head slightly, trying to discern what was there. Then the shape of a man stepped out from beside the woodpile and Bursofsky barely had time to draw his pistol before a thick chunk of wood in the man's hands swung upward into the side of the marshal's head, sending him sprawling onto the ground. The gun skidded across the alley into the bushes.

Clint McCall dropped the small log and leapt forward, eager to finish the marshal off while the latter was still vulnerable. His knees came down on Bursofsky's abdomen, and he heard him gasp as the air left his lungs. McCall brought his fist down hard into Bursofsky's face, splitting the skin just above the left eyebrow. Blood began to pour freely from the freshly opened wound.

McCall was sure he had him now. He pulled back his fist to deliver another blow. Bursofsky was fighting against unconsciousness, but he wasn't about to go down that easily. He brought his knee up between McCall's legs, using all his force to crush the man's testicles. McCall grunted in agony, sliding halfway off the lawman and steadying himself with his hand. Bursofsky delivered a right hook to McCall's head, hitting him hard in the left ear. The blow pushed the assassin entirely off Bursofsky, whose adrenaline was flowing mightily now.

Bursofsky scrambled to his hands and knees, still trying to get air back into his lungs. McCall thrust a boot toward his face, missing by inches. Bursofsky grasped his leg and twisted. A loud cracking sound came from McCall's ankle, and he used his other leg to kick Bursofsky squarely in the chest. Bursofsky tumbled over on his side, released his grip on McCall's injured ankle. Eyes watering with pain,

McCall sprang to his feet, weaving as he stood.

He slipped his knife from its sheath on his forearm, but Bursofsky wasn't finished yet. He kicked out wildly toward McCall, catching the man on the shins. McCall's feet flew out from under him and he hurtled face down onto the ground with a sickening thud. McCall blacked out momentarily, his lips split grotesquely and his two front teeth dangling by the roots. Blood filled his mouth as he struggled to stay alert. Remarkably, he still had the knife in his right hand.

Now Bursofsky was on his feet. He kicked McCall in the ribs and his hand groped toward his hip to pull his pistol. Then he realized that his gun was somewhere in the bushes across the alley. He knelt and reached for the stranger's gun. Neither man was operating at full consciousness, both having suffered serious blows to the head since the scuffle began. Bursofsky was fairly sure that his opponent was out cold as his fingers wrapped around the handle of the man's pistol.

In a final, desperate effort to finish off Bursofsky and move on before their fight attracted unwanted attention, McCall rolled over quickly and thrust the knife upwards into the marshal's chest. McCall hadn't had time to take aim, but the knife struck at exactly the most lethal spot. It plunged into Bursofsky's left breast, sinking straight into his heart. Bursofsky blinked a couple of times, and then blood streamed from between his lips. His impaled heart stopped beating, and McCall rolled out of the way as the dead weight of the marshal's body collapsed onto the ground.

McCall lifted himself to one elbow, breathing heavily as he gathered his wits. His ankle throbbed with pain, and he gingerly touched the broken teeth in his mouth. He looked at Bursofsky's body and cursed softly.

'You were a might tougher than you looked, Marshal,' he muttered under his breath respectfully. He hadn't expected anywhere near that much fight from the small-town badge-toter.

It took over two minutes before McCall was ready to get up. He knelt beside the corpse and searched the dead marshal's pockets. He quickly found what he was looking for, and put the keys in his coat pocket. He rose and began limping down the alley toward the rear of the jail.

13

Steve Karner was getting worried.

Marshal Ethan Bursofsky had been gone for well over an hour now. Karner knew that midnight must be drawing near, and that Ash would be on time, ready to pry through the board in the ceiling as they had discussed. But when he had conceived of his escape plan, Karner hadn't reckoned on the marshal still being up and around, wandering the streets. He could return anytime, and when he did, he would come in to make his final nightly check on the prisoner, as he invariably did before turning in.

Hell, thought Karner. He might just walk up on Ash climbing up to the roof. What would they do then?

He was pacing the floor of his cell, walking back and forth before the barred door. He was anxious, keenly aware that this was his last chance to get out before the district attorney arrived from Salem. Once that happened, everything was out of his hands. He had no idea whether Pete Taylor was still in town, but he assumed he was. If he was going to get his hands on Taylor, this was likely his final opportunity to do so.

The thought of Taylor getting away was almost more than Karner could bear. He was the key to everything — to the attempt on Karner's life, to the years Karner had spent wandering, and especially to the death of Patsy McCurtin. Taylor had told the men he had hired that he wanted Karner dead so that he could be with Patsy. Karner still questioned Taylor's motives on that point, but he had no doubt that that was what Taylor had told the five men he had turned into would-be murderers.

Yes — he had to get to Pete Taylor. Once that was done, the entire sordid affair would be behind him, and he could look to the future for the first time in years.

His thoughts were interrupted by the sound of scuffling on the wall at the back of his cell. It must be midnight, he thought, because Ash is here.

Five minutes later, Karner heard a soft tapping on the board in the ceiling. He moved directly under it.

He heard Ash's voice come through from the roof. 'You ready, boy?' the old man asked quietly.

Karner looked down the corridor toward the front office. This wasn't the ideal situation for his escape, but he would have to make do.

'I'm ready, Ash,' Karner said, cupping his hands on either side of his mouth. 'We got to make it fast, though, because the marshal ain't in his office.'

'He ain't?'

'Nope. He went out a couple hours ago and he hasn't come back yet. So let's get this done.'

'I'm on it,' Ash said.

Karner heard the sounds of objects

being moved on the roof, and then he heard wood creaking as his uncle pried it.

'They must have added a couple boards here,' said Ash.

Karner said nothing, his eyes still riveted on the cell block door. There was a cracking sound above him and Ash spoke again. 'Couple more minutes and we'll be in business.'

The sounds continued, the old man doing his best to be as quiet as he could.

There was a momentary lull in the activity on the roof, and Karner was horrified to hear the front door of the marshal's office being opened.

'Ash, for God's sake — he's coming!' Just as the words left his mouth, he heard another board being pried away up on the roof. Intent on his work, Ash didn't respond to Karner's warning.

He heard boots thumping across the planks of the office floor, moving toward the cell block. The gait was strange, as if the person were limping and dragging a foot. Karner heard the rattling of keys as the person in the office selected the proper one to unlock the connecting door.

'Almost done,' Ash called. He pulled at the last board as the key turned in the lock. The handle of the door turned and the hinges groaned as the door was pushed open.

The lantern dangling on the hook across from Karner's cell cast a bright light. Karner watched as a man limped into the corridor and shuffled toward him. The man's suit was expensive and tailored, but it was covered in dirt and part of one lapel was ripped. There were buttons missing from the man's fancy shirt. His face was swollen and his mouth bloodied. He stopped in front of the cell, glaring at Karner.

'Steve Karner?' he asked.

'Who the hell are you?' Karner retorted. 'And how did you get the marshal's keys?'

Clint McCall smiled sourly. 'You got a lot of sand,' he muttered, the awkward angle of his two front teeth making his speech slurred. He straightened. 'I'm afraid the marshal won't be joining us.' He coughed, wiping blood from his lips. 'I have to say, I've been hired for a lot of different jobs, but no one ever paid me as much as I'm getting to kill you.'

'Kill me?' Karner asked. He wasn't aware that the sounds of Ash's labors on the roof had ceased. 'Someone paid you to kill me?'

The brutal fight with Bursofsky was making McCall unusually loquacious. 'That's right,' he said. 'Quite a tidy sum, too. Of course, I had to take out a few others. Seems like killing you alone wasn't quite good enough. Feller really wanted to clean house.'

'Who is this feller?'

McCall grinned crookedly, pushing aside his coat on his right side, revealing the Colt pistol there. 'Lockhart,' he said simply. 'That's his name.'

Karner's face colored. 'Lockhart?'

The killer nodded. 'That's right.' His

hand gripped the butt of his pistol, but he hadn't drawn it yet.

A voice boomed from overhead. 'Steve!' Ash bellowed. Karner looked up to the ceiling. There was an opening there now, through which the twinkling stars were visible. A hand reached through, gripping a pistol. 'Take it, boy!'

Karner snapped into action. Ash dropped the pistol toward him and Karner caught it in his right hand. He saw movement in his peripheral vision and lowered his eyes to McCall, who had drawn his gun and raised it toward Karner. McCall fired, and Karner felt the bullet burn the side of his neck as it barely missed him. It smacked into the wall behind him, and then he knew exactly what to do.

He raised his uncle's Colt waist-high, and his left hand chopped at the hammer, sending one round after another into Clint McCall. McCall staggered, his pistol falling from his fingers and clattering on the floor. His glassy eyes met Karner's, and then his legs folded beneath him and he crashed onto the floor.

The smell of powder smoke was thick in the air, but Karner was scarcely conscious of it. He stood still, staring at the dead man before him, his mind in a daze. Ash leaned down and looked into the cell.

'Better him than you,' he said grimly. 'Hang on a minute — I'm coming down through the office.'

Karner nodded absently. He tossed the gun onto his bunk, trying to make sense of what the stranger had told him. There were sounds outside as Ash descended from the roof, and then he heard him coming through the office into the cell block.

Ash stared down at McCall's body. 'Who the hell is he?' he asked.

'I don't know,' Karner replied. 'He has the keys to the cell, though. Check his pockets.'

Ash knelt and felt for the keys, which he located in the dead man's left coat pocket. He stepped to the cell and unlocked it, pushing it open. Steve

Karner stepped into the corridor.

'Did you hear what he told me?' he asked.

'Not all of it,' Ash said.

'He said he was sent here to kill me by . . . Lockhart.'

Ash's bushy eyebrows darted upward. 'You sure?' he asked.

'I'm sure,' Karner said.

He crouched and felt the inside pockets of McCall's now blood-soaked coat. He removed a folded sheet of paper and opened it. The words were slightly smeared by the blood, and part of the sheet had been penetrated by one of the bullets that had killed Clint McCall. But the words were legible enough.

'What's it say?' Ash asked, staring down at the dead stranger on the floor. McCall's face seemed to be grimacing in death.

Karner read aloud, 'Taylor. Taylor. Bursofsky. Karner.'

'What's it mean?'

'I think — ' Karner began, and then hesitated. 'I think it's a list of people

189

this feller was hired to kill.'

'Good Lord,' Ash muttered.

'I have a feeling he's already killed the other three,' Karner said. 'For him to get the marshal's keys, he'd have to kill Bursofsky. The man wouldn't give them up willingly.'

'But why? Who would want these people dead?'

Karner's face was drawn. 'The person who set me up all those years ago, on the riverbank. That's who.' He dropped the note onto the floor beside the corpse. 'Lockhart.' He clenched his jaw as his mind put the pieces into place. 'And I think we know which Lockhart, too, Ash.'

'That little bastard Paul.'

'Yes, indeed. Paul.'

Without another word, Ash Karner unhitched his gun belt and handed it to his nephew. Steve Karner strapped it on, then stepped into the cell to retrieve the pistol from off the bunk. He carefully reloaded the gun and slipped it into the holster. His face bore an expression of determination and profound anger.

'I'm going over to the Lockhart place,' he said. 'See if you can find Bursofsky. If he's dead, he must be somewhere nearby.'

Ash nodded and followed Karner into the front office. Ash had left his rifle on the marshal's desk and he picked it up before they proceeded out onto the sidewalk. Standing there in the street was the bartender and a few of the patrons from the nearby saloon. The bartender was holding a shotgun.

The two Karners stopped and looked toward the men.

'What the hell is going on here?' the bartender asked.

'A hired killer just tried to shoot me in my cell,' Karner said. 'I think he already killed the marshal. He may have also killed Pete and Phil Taylor.' The men's faces reflected their skepticism, but Karner wasn't concerned about them. 'Now I'm going to take care of a little business. If any of you want to stand in my way, then make your move and make it quick. I ain't got time to waste.'

His eyes moved from face to face. No one wanted to take up his offer. He descended the steps into the street and walked past them toward Water Street and the home of the Lockhart family.

14

Water Street was engulfed in darkness as Karner turned onto it from Main. It was nearing one o'clock in the morning, and the respectable residents of Stayton's most exclusive street had long since turned in for the night. The next morning they would arise early, eager to get to work and accumulate more riches.

But not everyone would be rising early. Karner was going to see to that.

His boots sounded dully in the gravel as he made his way toward the end of the street. That's where the Lockharts lived — where the family had lived for more than thirty years. He came to the edge of their yard and looked the property over. Huge trees encircled it, and a lush green lawn filled the area between the trees and the house itself. Near where Karner was standing was an ornate gazebo that old Mrs Lockhart often sat in on warm days. She would spend hours there, knitting.

He could remember seeing her there when he was a boy. He often delivered packages from the general store. He could remember seeing Tom and Paul playing together in the back yard, a set of twins who had little in common apart from their appearance, and even there they were far from identical. Sometimes young Steve would take a break and play with them for a few minutes, but it was usually only Tom who would take the time to treat the poor orphaned boy like a friend and an equal. Paul frequently refused to play, or he would mock Karner's clothes.

Memories of those days came vividly to Karner as he stood beneath a massive maple tree, staring at the shadowy house. He hadn't thought of such things in twenty years, but it was almost as if he were a kid again, working hard at his summer job to help bring in a little extra money for his uncle and himself. He realized just how much of his childhood had been entangled with the Lockharts. Their power and influence utterly dominated Stayton and the area around the small town.

He moved out from under the tree and walked along the edge of the yard toward the back porch. Not a single light shone from inside the house. He knew where Paul's room was located. It was at the rear of the house, on the first floor. Karner quietly climbed the steps and twisted the knob on the back door. To his surprise, it opened.

He stepped through into the kitchen. The only light was from the moon outside, but he could see well enough. He passed into the dining room and glanced down the short hallway to his left. That's where Paul Lockhart kept his room. He turned and walked toward the door, the thick rug muting the sound of his boots. He saw that the door was partially open, and he drew his pistol before cautiously leaning over and looking inside. There was no one in the room. The bed was neatly made, and there was a towel folded on the dresser next to a basin and a large water pitcher. The room looked like it hadn't been used in some time. Wherever Paul Lockhart was, it wasn't here.

Karner left the room and moved back down the hallway. He turned left into the dining room and walked through to the parlor beyond. The curtains were drawn here and Karner paused in the doorway. He inhaled sharply when he saw the shape of a man sitting in a chair across the room. He couldn't make out the man's features, but the person was clearly looking back at him. He raised his pistol and pointed it at the dark form in the chair.

'That you, Paul?' he asked quietly. 'We got some talking to do.'

'Good evening, Steve,' a voice replied. 'What brings you here?'

Karner frowned. 'Tom?' he asked.

A match sprang to life and moved toward a lantern on the table by the chair. The lantern took flame and the person blew out the match before turning up the wick. It was Tom Lockhart, dressed in his pajamas, a large tumbler of whiskey sitting beside the lamp on the table. He smiled benignly at Karner.

'I thought you were in jail,' he said. 'Did the marshal let you out?'

'Not quite,' Karner said, lowering his gun.

'I'm a little confused, Steve. What's going on? Why are you here with that pistol?'

Karner slipped it into leather, suddenly aware of what a threatening presence he must seem. He didn't want Tom Lockhart to be afraid — he was here for Paul, not his brother.

'I'm looking for Paul,' Karner said thinly. 'He and I need to talk.'

'What about?' asked Lockhart, a furrow creasing his brow.

'It's a personal matter,' Karner said. 'Between me and him.'

'Sounds serious. Well, I'm sorry to say that Paul isn't here. He went down to Medford for a few days. He'll be back Tuesday afternoon.'

Karner's frustration was intense. 'Damn. That's too bad.' He rubbed his hands together. 'Medford, you say?'

Lockhart nodded. 'He went to see our uncle and aunt. They own some property down there that he wants to buy from them.'

'I see,' Karner said. The situation wasn't one for which he was prepared, but that was true of virtually everything that had transpired tonight. He heaved a heavy sigh. 'You mind if I sit down, Tom?'

Lockhart gestured toward a plush velvet chair about five feet from where Karner stood. 'Try that one,' he said helpfully. 'It's very comfortable, and you look like you've been rode hard and put away wet, if you don't mind my saying so.'

Karner walked to the chair and sank down on its soft seat. He leaned back and rubbed his eyes. 'What a goddamn night,' he said.

'How so?' Lockhart inquired, taking a sip from his tumbler.

Karner examined a stain on the leg of his pants for a moment before responding. 'I guess you're going to find everything out soon enough, so my telling you don't make all that much of a difference,' he opined. 'You see, a man tried to kill me in my cell tonight, just like five men tried to kill me on the riverbank three years ago. Like them, he failed to complete his duty. And also like them, the feller was hired to kill me by . . . ' He hesitated, but only for a moment. 'By your brother.'

There was an odd twitching in one corner of Tom Lockhart's mouth.

'My brother?' he asked. 'Paul hired someone to kill you?'

'Twice, it appears,' said Karner deliberately.

'Why would he do that?'

'That's what I wanted to ask him. Pete Taylor set it all up for him. I got a message that night, three years ago. It said Patsy needed to see me at the swimming hole east of town. That she wanted to meet at quarter to midnight.

So I went. I'd never gotten a letter like that from her before, so I knew it had to be serious. I thought she was in some kind of trouble.'

'What kind of trouble could Patsy McCurtin get into?' Lockhart asked. 'She was a straight-laced girl.'

Karner spread his hands. 'I know. That's why I headed out there. I thought maybe one of her brothers was in trouble again and she wanted me to help him out. It had happened before — like that time they got drunk and were out tipping cows at the Ackler farm. Remember that?'

'Dimly,' Lockhart said. His face looked slightly amused. 'They were always up to something, those McCurtin boys. I don't remember it ever being serious, though.'

'No, it wasn't. They just liked to play around and have fun. I thought maybe that was why she had sent me the note — I figured one of them was drunk at the swimming hole or something like that. I really didn't know what to think, to tell you the truth. But I wasn't going to leave Patsy hanging if she needed me.'

'Of course not.'

'I got out there at quarter to midnight on the dot. I know because I had my pa's old watch on me and checked it when I tied my horse. Next thing I know, Jack Buckley comes strolling out of the trees. A minute later, Norm Ballard, Clarence Snow, Gil Thompson, and Dave Villiers showed up. Every one of them was three sheets to the wind. They started talking all friendly, asking me what I was doing there and such. Then Jack hit me with a rock and they all joined in.'

Lockhart shook his head mournfully and took another sip of his whiskey. 'Lord have mercy,' he said. 'Why would they do that?'

'Because they were paid to,' Karner said. 'And in a couple of cases, probably because they'd wanted to do it for years. They beat me to within an inch of my life and then threw me in the river with my hands tied. I damn near drowned.'

'But you didn't.'

'No. Don't know how I didn't, but I didn't. Got nursed back to health by an old lady near Salem. That's when I read about Patsy. Didn't much feel like coming back home after that.'

'Where did you go?'

'A lot of places, but I spent most of my time in Idaho, just thinking about what had happened. It just didn't make sense to me — none of it. Even now, I don't know what to make of it, but I know a lot more about why it happened than I did before.'

'How does it all tie in with Paul?'

'Like I said, it never really made sense to me that Pete Taylor would want to do this to me, especially over Patsy. He never showed the slightest interest in Patsy his whole life. But every single one of the four flushers who attacked me told me the same thing — that Pete Taylor paid them and told them what to do. He threatened to fire them from the mill if they didn't do it. He also threatened to burn them out of their homes.'

Lockhart leaned forward. 'Pete Taylor told them he'd have them fired from the Lockhart mill?' Karner nodded. 'He didn't have any say over who worked there. He was just blowing smoke.'

'Maybe,' Karner replied. 'Or maybe there was someone behind the whole thing who did have some say about whether those fellers kept their jobs or not.'

'You mean . . . Paul?'

'That's how it looks.'

'But why would Paul do all this?'

'Your guess is as good as mine,' Karner said, glancing around the room. 'I know a feller either killed the marshal tonight or hurt him badly. Somehow he got his hands on Bursofsky's keys and tried to shoot me dead in my cell. Luckily Ash was there to lend me a hand, or else I'd be a goner. Before he met his maker, the feller decided to say a few words.'

'He did?' asked Lockhart with a

raised eyebrow. It all seemed to be too much for him to take in.

'Yes, he did.'

'What did he say?'

'That a man named Lockhart had hired him.'

'I see.'

'Kind of interesting that Paul would be out of town on the night this killer comes to settle the score,' Karner observed.

'I hadn't thought of that,' said Lockhart, draining the rest of his whiskey. He sighed and placed his hands in his lap. 'What is it you plan on doing when you track Paul down?'

'Talk, first. What happens then depends on what he has to say.' He gazed at Tom Lockhart's face from across the room. 'You understand why I need to do this, don't you?'

'I understand,' said Lockhart. 'I suppose anyone would feel the way you do, after everything you've been through. And if my brother was responsible, then he certainly has some explaining to do.'

'I'm glad you're not taking this personal, Tom.'

'Well, even if I were, what could I do about it?'

'Nothing, really. It's between me and Paul now.'

'Losing a girl like Patsy would drive any man to do things he'd never thought he could do,' Lockhart asserted. 'There really aren't a lot of girls like her around.'

'You can say that again,' Karner said.

'When she died — well, it was one of the worst days of my entire life,' Lockhart continued. His voice was oddly flat and metallic. 'I loved Patsy very much. Always had.'

A vaguely uneasy feeling came over Karner. 'Well, she always cared about you, too, Tom. You were a good friend to her.'

'Right,' Lockhart said. 'A . . . good friend.'

Karner chose his words carefully, suddenly aware that a strange new atmosphere had settled over the conversation. 'It's funny, though — I never knew Paul to take much of an interest in Patsy. Kind of like Pete Taylor.'

Lockhart's face was expressionless. 'That's true.'

'It's a strange thing.'

'What's strange, Steve?'

'That Paul and Pete would set me up to be killed,' Karner said, his body taut and his senses alert, 'and that the men they hired to do the job for them would think it was over Patsy.'

That odd twitch was back at the corner of Tom Lockhart's lips. 'Yes,' he said. 'That's very strange.'

He raised his right hand from his lap. In it he held a shiny silver Derringer, both barrels of which were pointed at Steve Karner.

15

The light from the lantern glinted off the small pistol. Karner knew Tom Lockhart was a good shot, and either of the .41 caliber bullets were more than enough to kill him where he sat. He silently cursed his own naiveté — his mind had been reeling after the encounter with the killer at the jail, and when he heard the name 'Lockhart', only one of the two brothers had seemed capable of being behind all of this. And it hadn't been Tom.

But it *was* Tom. It had been Tom all along.

'What are you doing with that gun, Tom?' Karner asked.

'I'm pointing it at you, Steve,' Lockhart said, his affect still bizarrely detached. 'You are a very dangerous man, as I think you've amply demonstrated ever since you came back to town.'

'I guess I should apologize, Tom.'

'What for, Steve?'

'For impugning your brother's good name.'

Lockhart laughed at that one. 'Oh, yes — poor Paul. He'd be devastated.' He chuckled again. 'Actually, Paul would never have had the guts to do what I did. He's never loved anyone in his entire life but himself. I only did what I did because of my love for Patsy.'

'That right?' Karner asked, careful to keep his tone neutral.

'Of course it's right, you imbecile. You're kind of like Paul in that respect. You never think of anyone but yourself.'

'I've always considered you a friend, Tom. I don't think I've ever done you wrong.'

Lockhart snorted disdainfully. 'You've never done me right, either. If it weren't for you, I'd be married to Patsy right now.'

Karner tried to suppress the rage that was rising steadily within him as he listened to Lockhart speak. 'You think so?'

'I know so.'

'So that's what all this has been about, huh? All the planning, all the killing. You wanted Patsy for yourself, and then when that didn't work out, you wanted to cover your trail.'

'That about sums it up, old friend.' Lockhart's face showed his indifference to Karner's judgment. 'You never deserved Patsy. She was a woman of refinement. A rare beauty. There was depth to her. She deserved better than to marry some orphan who would never be able to give her the life that I would have given her. But nothing would change the way she felt about you. The more I think about it — and I've thought about it quite a bit, as you can imagine — the more I think that Patsy's biggest flaw was loyalty. She was never able to see past the things she had cherished as a child.'

'Patsy cared about you, Tom. She always treated you like a friend.'

'True, true. I can't dispute that. She always treated me like a . . . *friend*.'

Lockhart almost spat the last word out. 'Meanwhile, she was busy planning on marrying you and throwing her entire life away, living in some two-bit cabin and working herself to the bone.' His grip on the Derringer tightened until his knuckles were white. 'Not to mention wasting her best years bearing you one little brat after another. I always noticed how you looked at her. You were like some dirty animal, just waiting to put your filthy paws on her.'

'I guess you think if someone was going to touch her, it should have been you.'

'You got that right. I would have given her a life beyond her wildest dreams. A life you could never have imagined, with your limited breeding and your tiny mind.'

'You know, you're right, Tom,' said Karner. 'You are a much more refined and educated man than I could ever be. But I think there's one thing you've overlooked.'

'Oh? And what's that?'

'You're the reason Patsy's dead, you sorry sack of shit!'

With those words, Karner dived to the right, overturning the chair in which he was sitting. The Derringer fired just a second too late, the bullets exploding into the wall rather than Karner's head.

Steve Karner landed in the doorway to the dining room and quickly crawled through on his hands and knees. He drew his pistol and leaned back against the wall, listening for sounds from the other room. He heard rapid movements and the sound of a table being knocked over and something crashing onto the floor, as if Lockhart were running from the parlor.

'Run as fast as you want, you bushwhacking son of a bitch!' Karner called. 'I'm coming for you. You won't be able to hide from me!'

He heard the sound of someone moving in one of the rooms at the front of the massive Lockhart house. He figured Tom Lockhart was either in his father's library or in the sitting room by the front staircase. He took it for granted that the man was arming himself with more than just the little Derringer he had used in the parlor.

A woman's voice abruptly echoed through the foyer of the house. Karner recognized it instantly as that of Ethel Lockhart, the family matriarch.

'Thomas?' she called. 'What's happened? I thought I heard a gun.'

Karner listened for Lockhart to answer his mother. He could still hear someone moving beyond the parlor. Lockhart didn't respond to his mother's anxious query.

'Thomas?' she called again. Once more there was no response from her son.

Karner rose and peered around the doorway into the parlor. A table near the opposite door had been overturned, and a large, expensive-looking vase was in shattered pieces on the hardwood floor. He entered the parlor and moved swiftly toward the other doorway, careful to avoid stepping on the chunks of porcelain. He leaned forward and glanced beyond into the foyer. It was dark there, the only light coming from the silvery moon outside.

Again Mrs Lockhart spoke, her quavering voice fearful. 'Thomas, please! If you don't answer me, I'm coming down there.'

'I wouldn't do that, Mrs Lockhart,' Karner called. 'There's likely to be some gunplay down here. I think you should go back to your room and lock the door.'

'Who is that?' she cried.

A shotgun blast from the doorway of the library sent chunks of marble and stone raining down onto the shiny floor of the foyer. The blast had hit the wall about five feet from where Karner stood. Tom Lockhart was letting Karner know that he had, indeed, reinforced himself.

Karner heard Mrs Lockhart's steps as she hurried back across the landing on the second floor. Then he heard a door slam shut and knew that she was back in her room, as he had suggested.

'She's gone now, Tom,' he called. 'It's just you and me. Who do you figure is going to come out of this alive?'

There was no reply. Karner waited a few more seconds and then dove into the foyer, rolling across the floor and coming up in a crouching position, his big Navy Colt in his right hand. He saw a shadow move in the library across the foyer and fired at it. He missed, but he had Tom Lockhart on the run and trapped in the library. He tried to remember if there was a door in that room that led outside, but he wasn't sure if he had ever been in there or if he had just looked into the room during his visits to the house as a kid.

Still crouching, he cat-footed over to the wall and moved along it toward the library doorway. There was no movement in the room as he looked in, but he knew Lockhart was in there somewhere.

'Hey, Tom,' he called. 'After I killed that sidewinder you hired, I checked his pockets and found a little list. It had four names on it. You had the Taylor brothers killed. I can understand killing Pete, but why Phil?'

A laugh erupted from within the library. 'Pete liked to talk,' Lockhart said. 'I couldn't take the chance that he'd told Phil everything.'

'Makes sense, I guess,' Karner replied, and then leapt through the doorway, firing a couple of shots toward the rear of the library where he had heard Lockhart's voice. He didn't expect to hit him, but he wanted to create a distraction and provide cover. He heard one slug hit the wall; the other shattered a large window, the pane of glass collapsing down onto the library floor with a thunderous crash.

Karner heard boots crunching over the glass. He sat up just in time to see Lockhart slip out of the library into the garden beside it. Karner rose and aimed quickly. He fired and Lockhart screamed, collapsing into the grass and dropping his shotgun. Karner moved across the room to the window; cold air flowed in where the glass had been. He fired another shot through the window into the garden, and hurled himself through, landing on the stones of the large patio.

He was disoriented for a moment. He looked up to see Lockhart standing above him, swinging the barrels of the shotgun at his head. He tried to raise the pistol and fire but he was a second too late. The gun smashed against the side of his head and he saw dazzling colors and then darkness. He fought against it, forcing himself to remain awake. Lockhart snarled and tried to strike him again with the gun, but Karner dropped his pistol and gripped the shotgun barrel, shoving himself upward to his feet.

Their faces were inches apart as they struggled over the gun. Lockhart was about the same size as Karner, and nearly as strong. Karner's last shot had hit Lockhart in the thigh, but in his murderous frenzy he seemed largely

216

unaffected by the wound. His lips were pulled back from his teeth as he fought for the weapon.

'It's over, Tom,' Karner said. 'You're going to die tonight. You've earned it.'

They pushed against each other, trying to twist the shotgun from the other's hands. Lockhart lunged forward, bashing his forehead against Karner's nose. There was an audible crunch as the cartilage broke, and blood began to pour out over his mouth and chin. Still Karner didn't break his grip on the gun.

A voice called out from the frame of the shattered window. From the corner of his eye, Karner spotted an elderly man standing there, a pistol in his hand.

'Stop!' the man cried, his pistol extended toward the struggling duo. Karner realized that it was Edward Lockhart, the ruler of the family empire.

'Shoot him, Pa!' Tom Lockhart yelled. 'Kill this bastard! He shot the marshal and now he's trying to kill me!'

Karner was briefly distracted, and the younger Lockhart shoved him backward, breaking his grip on the shotgun. Karner fell onto the patio. He glanced at Edward Lockhart, who now pointed his pistol at Karner as if to fire. Karner braced himself for the impact of the bullet, but when a shot sounded it came not from the library window but from the trees on the other side of the garden.

Blood spurted from Edward Lockhart's chest and he fell backward into the library. Ash Karner stepped out of the shadows, smoke rising from the muzzle of his Winchester rifle. Tom Lockhart stepped forward, ready to bring down the shotgun on Karner's head again, but his quarry had fallen only a foot away from where he had dropped his pistol. Steve Karner palmed the Navy Colt and raised it toward Lockhart, who froze in his tracks, the shotgun raised.

'When you get to hell,' Karner said, 'say hello to Pete Taylor and all the boys for me.' He fired two shots into the center of Tom Lockhart's chest. 'Those are for Patsy and the marshal.'

In the moonlight, the blood that flowed from the holes looked black. Lockhart dropped the shotgun and it clattered onto the stones of the patio. Remarkably, he remained on his feet, wheezing as the blood filled his lungs. He clawed at his shirt, almost as if he hoped to pull the bullets from his chest. He raised his eyes and met Karner's gaze for a moment. Then the eyes rolled back in his head and he dropped to the patio in an untidy heap.

Ash Karner raced across the grass and jumped up onto the patio. He reached down and helped his nephew to his feet. He put his arm around the younger man's shoulders and helped steady him.

'It's all done now, boy,' he said. 'All done.'

16

The next day, the sheriff came to Stayton. He brought with him a deputy whom he assigned as the interim town marshal until the mayor and town council found someone to replace Ethan Bursofsky.

Steve Karner voluntarily allowed himself to be taken into custody, and at last the full story of what had happened to him and who had conceived and organized it was told to the proper authorities. With both Tom and Edward Lockhart dead, the family's influence was severely diminished, although Paul Lockhart did his best to turn the sheriff against Karner. In the end, however, there was too much evidence leading back to Tom Lockhart, and the confirmation of Clint McCall's identity and of Lockhart's transfer of several thousand dollars to McCall's bank marked the end of the investigation. The charges over the attack on Phil Taylor were quietly forgotten.

There was insufficient evidence to charge Steve Karner with the murders of Clarence Snow, Gil Thompson, Norm Ballard, or Dave Villiers. No witnesses had seen him with the men, let alone seen him kill them. The sheriff had no doubt that Karner was responsible for their deaths, but declined to go further than telling Karner so.

'I know you did it, Karner,' he said. 'And so do you. But I can't bring you to trial for it. So I guess we'll just call it even.' He folded his arms across his chest. 'Besides, those fellers did their part to earn what they got. That's all there is to it.'

He released Karner on a cold morning in late November. Ash was waiting for him on the steps outside the marshal's office, and there were several townspeople gathered on the sidewalk to see him. There was still a sense of shock and disbelief among the residents of Stayton, but their sentiments were firmly on the side of Steve Karner.

Mack McCurtin put his gnarled hand on Karner's shoulder and smiled. 'You did good, son,' he said.

'Patsy deserved nothing less,' Karner replied.

McCurtin nodded, then mounted his horse and rode out in the direction of his home. Someone brought Karner's horse from the livery. He put a foot in a stirrup and heaved up into the saddle. Ash mounted his horse and together they rode out to the old man's cabin.

That night after supper, Karner rode out to the cemetery. It was a moonless, overcast night, with a layer of mist covering the ground. He alighted near Patsy's grave and removed his hat.

'I got them, Patsy,' he said softly. 'They won't ever be able to hurt anyone else again. And they paid for what they did to you and me. I made a promise when you died that as long as there was breath in me, I wouldn't stop until I righted the wrongs that had been done to us. It took me a little while, but I kept my promise. So now you can rest in peace.'

He replaced his hat and rode away, knowing he would never again visit her grave. He was done with Stayton — done with the betrayals, the bloodshed and death, the dark secrets that he had unveiled in his relentless quest to exact vengeance for himself and the woman he loved. He was done with the past. It was as if his life was a book, and this chapter was complete, never to be revisited. He could move forward now, at last.

Karner returned to the cabin and slept soundly. He awoke the next morning to find Ash boiling coffee and making eggs and bacon. He had a flashback to his childhood, when so many mornings had begun in exactly this same fashion. He sat up and pushed some of the hair away from his forehead, watching the old man. There seemed to be a new spring in Ash's step. He had his nephew back, and now he knew he wasn't going to be charged with murder and possibly hanged. Karner smiled, and then just as quickly the smile faded, for he knew he would have to tell Ash he was leaving again.

He rose and they ate in comfortable silence. Finally, Karner broached the subject.

'Ash,' he said. 'I'm going to be leaving again.'

Ash kept his eyes on his plate and pushed a piece of bacon into his mouth. Then he nodded.

'Yeah, I figured you would,' he said. 'This ain't the same town it was when you was little. Too much water under the bridge, if you know what I'm saying.'

'I do. And you're exactly right. There's nothing for me here anymore, except you, of course.'

'Where you heading to, boy?' Ash asked.

'Oh, I don't know. I was thinking maybe California. Never been there before, but I heard a man can make a good life there if he's willing to work for it.'

Ash wiped his mouth. 'You ain't never been afraid of work, that's for damn sure.'

'Well, I learned from you. You're probably the hardest working man I ever knew.'

Ash grinned. 'Hell, your pa could work me under the table any day of the week, and I ain't just saying that.'

Karner ate, thinking of what Ash would do with himself from now on. A thought occurred to him.

'Ash, why don't you come along with me?' he asked. 'You're still healthy as an ox, and you deserve to see a little of the world. Come on down to California with me. The two of us together could make our way with no problems.'

Ash Karner looked up, his face beaming. 'You mean it, Steve? You don't think an old codger like me would slow you down?'

'Hell yes, I mean it! And you wouldn't slow me down a bit, Ash. I can't think of anyone else I'd rather ride with than you.'

Ash wiped up some egg yolk with a crust of bread and washed it down with a large gulp of hot coffee. He looked around his sparse cabin — the place where he had lived for the vast majority of his nearly seventy years of life. Karner wondered if his uncle was having second thoughts about leaving.

'You sure you could leave this place behind?' he asked.

Ash scoffed. 'Hell, this shack is just a place where I laid my head for a while. If you and me are riding together, then I'll feel at home no matter where we are.'

'Glad to hear it, Ash,' Karner said, fighting back emotions. 'I'm damn glad to hear it.'

A few hours later, Ash and Steve Karner rode out of the yard, heading west toward Salem. From there they planned to head south, all the way to California.